NO ONE HAS TO KNOW

RD BAKER

A NOTE FROM THE AUTHOR

This book is a love letter to my younger self.

I had always grown up being told that boys my age would never hold any interest for me. I was far too mature. I would most definitely end up with a much older man who was more in tune with my super mature self.

When I turned 18, and quickly caught the attention of a much older man, it went about as well as you can imagine. Being the hot young cash cow of an unemployed ex-heroin addict who pawned all my shit whenever he wanted to go on a shopping spree was not entirely what I had in mind when picturing my future, and it got old (haha, pun intended) quickly.

Yes, I dumped him. Yes, I moved on to many more medi-ocre men my age before finally meeting my husband (who is a whole ten months older than me).

But No One Has To Know is the love I dreamed of all those years ago when I was young, and inexperienced, and just wanting someone to take care of me.

Theo is the man I wish I had met. Theo is the kind of

man every young woman wanting a fun flirtation with an older man should encounter.

Theo is me reclaiming my past. And Amber got the life we all deserve.

So, enjoy this story, and may the myth that girls mature faster than boys finally die and allow us to find a love that is all-consuming, calming, and safe.

CONTENT NOTE

This book contains a large age gap between the MCs. There was no physical contact or romantic interaction between the MCs before the events of this book.

This book also contains themes of kink exploration, impact play, light degradation, themes of sharing, voyeurism, free use and somnophilia. All actions are discussed, consensual and take place between adults in a safe environment.

This book is not intended as an instruction manual and all kinks and fetishes when exercised in real life should always be done after research and discussion.

Play safe, be safe, and have fun!

For Deana

*I know I didn't quite manage a novella, but I still broke my
writing slump, so win?
I owe you all the queso
xxx*

1

FRIDAY AFTERNOON

There are days where I really miss being married. I miss the closeness, the intimacy that builds up knowing someone so closely you know what they look like when they brush their teeth. The inside jokes that don't even need words, just a shared glance across a crowded room that have you both laughing til you're crying.

And yes, the sex.

The sex with my ex-wife was never the problem. Even in the dying years of our marriage, in amongst the petty arguments and microaggressions, we still fucked regularly. Maybe hating each other even made the sex hotter?

That's messed up, right?

Coming home to an empty house every night, that sucks too. The silence gets to me sometimes. Lying in an empty bed is the pits. And on those nights where you've jerked off to yet more porn, and you feel like a washed-up loser, you can't help but question whether or not becoming single was the worst decision of your life.

But right now, watching my ex-wife fuss and fume over the trunk of her car, stacking suitcases and holding out an irritated hand the second I move anywhere near close enough to help, I'm reminded that maybe being divorced isn't all that bad.

"Theo, stop infantilizing me. I have got this, my *god*," Mella snaps, and I lean back against the door of my house with a shrug.

"No one's infantilizing you, we're just trying to help," I say, and meet my daughter's eyes. Laurie rolls them obligingly, her manicured fingers gripping the top of the car door as she hovers, waiting for her mother to finish packing so they can leave.

"Mom, just put some on the back seat," Laurie says, and Mella throws back her head with a flash of shiny black hair.

"And you're just as bad as *him*." That accusatory finger darts in my direction again.

"Well, she is right," I say, pointing to the suitcases that will not bend to my ex-wife's whim no matter how much she punches and prods. "It's not like anyone's sitting in the back."

Mella's face flushes red, and she pushes her hair from her brow, which is sweaty despite the cool fall breeze that's sprung up.

"I am actually picking someone up in Vermont, if you must know." She inhales heavily through her nose and fixes me with her big blue eyes. "I'm taking him to meet my parents this weekend."

Ah. That explains the mood.

Laurie's gaze flashes to mine with mild alarm, but I simply smile and shrug.

"Mella, for the love of all things holy, let me pack the damn trunk before you're forced to meet your new beau with chipped nails." I give her a warm smile, the one that always had her grinning and blushing when we were together, and even now, as she's tense and anxious, her shoulders relax and her jaw visibly unclenches. With a sigh and a wave of her hand, she gestures to the trunk.

"Fine. You were always better at these things than me." She stands back, crossing her arms over her chest, watching critically as I shift the suitcases, turning them so they're all standing side-on.

"The trunk will never close like-" Mella's critical gaze drops as I close the trunk with a loud thud. "That." She exhales heavily, then quickly fixes her face with a smile. "Thank you."

"Any time." I stand back, tucking my hands into the pockets of my jeans. "Now, you better hit the road or you'll get caught in all that traffic."

"Traffic?" Laurie asks, wrinkling her nose. "Why would there be traffic?"

"Fall colors, peanut." I gesture at the surrounding trees, brilliant red and gold leaves swishing softly in the breeze. "There'll be tourists everywhere."

"Great." Laurie grimaces, then quickly leaves her place by the car to wrap me in one last hug. "You sure you'll be OK? I feel bad leaving when I just got home."

"I'll be fine." I run a hand over her blonde hair, and kiss her forehead. "I'll see you when you get back next week. Your grandparents will be dying to hear all about how you're doing at college."

"Alright. But next week when I get back, it's you, me and apple pie at Stanton's."

I laugh and nod. "It's a date."

Laurie presses another quick kiss to my cheek, heading back to the car and throwing me a wave before dropping into her seat.

Mella turns to me with an uncertain look, tucking her

shoulder-length hair behind her ear. "I feel bad that I'm taking her away from you."

"You're not taking her away, she's been dying to go see your parents."

Mella looks over her shoulder at the car, and sighs softly. "Can you believe our girl's in her second year of college?"

"Nope. Yesterday she was a toddler who wouldn't let go of my legs the minute I walked in the door."

Mella laughs softly, turning back to me with a shake of her head. "Time sure flies."

"Yes, it does."

We gaze at each other, and for just a second, maybe we both see the people we were all those years ago, when our family was small and new. Before the yelling and the arguing and the finger-pointing started. But it passes quickly, as it always does, and now we're just two people in our mid-40s, looking at someone we once loved, but who is now as good as a stranger.

Weird feeling.

I clear my throat and nod at the car. "Go on, you've got a drive ahead of you." I raise my eyebrows with a smile. "And someone waiting on you."

"He's nice." Mella seems surprised that she said that, and quickly averts her gaze.

"I'm glad." And I'm not even lying. I am glad.

Mella mutters a quick *Bye*, and darts to her car, dropping into her seat and gunning the engine. Before she's left the driveway, music starts to blare from the car's speakers, and I can't help but grin when I recognize one of Laurie's latest K-Pop obsessions. The sound fades into the distance as they drive down my street, and then I'm alone in my drive again.

Yes, I'm glad. And maybe also a little jealous.

The sun is streaming into my kitchen, and I stand bare-foot on the hardwood floor as I pour myself a coffee. I look out at the trees that border my yard, and wonder what I should do for the rest of the afternoon. I have papers to grade, and a thesis to work on. And I should really hit the gym. Laurie's arrival a few days ago completely up-ended my workout routine, and I am way too old to not notice taking a few days off.

Getting older really sucks sometimes.

The doorbell surprises me, and with a laugh I head down the hall. Of course Laurie forgot something. She always does. Like clockwork.

I open the door, ready to chide her with a, *You'd forget your head if it wasn't screwed on,* and stop short. Because it's not Laurie at the door. It's a pretty young woman with long, coppery-auburn hair and light brown eyes, a big smile on her face.

"Amber, what are you doing here?"

Amber shrugs, her hands tucked away behind her back. "I was kind of hoping to see Laurie if she's home, too."

"Sorry, honey, you just missed her." I gesture down the street. "She's gone to Connecticut with her mom, to see her grandparents."

"Oh, shoot." Amber frowns, puffing out a sigh. "I've missed her so much. We've only been able to FaceTime a few times since we went back."

I regard my daughter's best friend with sympathy. "Oh, that's too bad, honey. She'll be back Tuesday though."

Amber's face brightens. "Great! Maybe I can see her then."

"I am sure she will make time for you." I expect this young woman to say a friendly goodbye, and flounce off down my drive in her short skirt and thigh-high socks. But she doesn't. She just stands there, smiling at me.

"You doing anything exciting this weekend?" She asks.

I lean against the door frame and shake my head. "Not really, just going to be hanging out at home, maybe heading to the gym. You know, exciting old guy stuff."

Amber rolls her eyes with a giggle. "You are *not* old."

The compliment sounds nice coming from a woman who just celebrated her 20th birthday, but I laugh and shake my head. "I am disgustingly old compared to you, and do disgustingly boring things accordingly."

"I have never seen an old man with muscles like yours," Amber counters, and quickly bites her lip. "Sorry, that probably sounded a little forward."

Goddamn, this girl is gonna make me blush. *You need to get out more, old man.* I wave my hand dismissively with an embarrassed chuckle.

"Hey, coming from a pretty girl like you, I'll take it." I take a sip of my coffee to stop myself from saying anything else that could be even creepier. "And you? You and your parents doing anything exciting this weekend?"

"My parents are out of town." Amber tugs on the sleeve of her rusty brown sweater, pulling it down over her wrist. "My brother has some giant football game in Boston, so they've all gone down for that."

"You didn't want to go?"

Amber wrinkles her nose and shakes her head. "I hate football. And I hate Boston."

"Fair enough." My feet are getting cold, and as much as talking to someone is nice, I know I should let this girl go and have fun. "Well, you take care, honey. I'll tell Laurie to call you when she gets home."

"Uh, Mr Rembrook," Amber says quickly as I take a step

back into my house. "Before I went to college you mentioned some books that you thought would be useful, engineering textbooks I think? But then I totally flaked and forgot to come get them. Could we, I don't know, only if I'm not bothering you, but could I maybe come in and grab those?" Her big brown eyes gaze up at me, lined with thick black lashes, and god, when did this girl turn from a gangly teenager singing too loud in my kitchen into the young woman in front of me? Time really flew. *Yes, Theo, she was a teenager in your kitchen a few years ago. Fucking stop ogling her. Pervert.*

"Of course, honey, come on in. Let me get them for you." I stand aside, letting her pass. I close the door behind us, following her as she walks through the house she knows probably as well as her own, and takes a left into my office.

She sighs happily as she walks in, and takes a deep breath.

"I always loved this room," she says, walking over to the shelves that line the walls, running her finger along a line of history books. "I used to talk Laurie into asking you to let us do our homework here."

I laugh softly, perching on the edge of my desk, and watch her walk around. "I remember, you two sprawled out here on the floor with your millions of books."

"Feels like a lifetime ago." She sounds so wistful I can't help but smile.

"Wait til you're my age, when you have a memory that spans back way more than 30 years."

Amber flashes me a smile and shakes her head. "You really need to stop talking about how old you are, because you're not that old." Her eyes drop to the floor, and her cheeks blush pink. "Laurie used to hate it, but we all talked about you being the Hot Dad."

I laugh out loud, covering my embarrassment. "You did not."

"We did. We all used to watch you jogging around the neighborhood with no shirt on." Amber lifts her eyes again with a grin, covering her face with her hands. "I can't believe I just admitted that to you."

"Hey, with any luck Alzheimer's will kick in by this afternoon and I'll forget."

Amber drops her hands with a roll of her eyes. "Mr Rembrook, stop it."

"Please call me Theo," I say, lifting my hands. "Mr Rembrook makes me feel like I'm back in a lecture hall."

"Ok, *Theo*." She drawls my name, eyes fixed directly on mine.

That felt like flirting. I give myself an internal slap. *Goddammit, what has gotten into you?*

"So, how's college?" I ask quickly, desperate to change the subject and to stop thinking about these pretty brown eyes gazing at my face.

Amber sighs, but this time it isn't a happy sound. She twirls a strand of copper hair around her finger, turning back to gaze up and down the bookshelf.

"It's fine. I have good professors, and I kind of like it all more than I thought I would." She takes a green and gold bound book from the shelf, turning so I can see her profile, and flips through the pages. "Architecture is kind of wild. I discovered I like bridges."

"Bridges, huh?"

She meets me with a smile, and nods. "How they're built, and everything that goes into deciding what will stay up and what will fall. You think a bridge is just, like, Point A to Point B. But it's so much more than that."

"Amber Pope, future Bridge Builder?" I laugh as she blushes. "Sounds good to me."

"Yeah, well, I can hope I guess." She looks over at me. "And how about you?"

"Same as always," I reply with a shrug. "Classes are classes. But I am working on my PhD, so..." I don't know what else to say to this bright young woman to make my boring, middle-aged life sound any more interesting, so I just shrug again.

"Are you seeing anyone?"

I'm sure my face betrays just how much that question, coming from Amber, throws me. I try to stutter out a reply, in the face of this young woman who is just gazing at me with soft eyes.

"Uh... Uh, I, um, no. I haven't really, uh..." I almost choke on my damn spit trying to swallow and wet my throat, but Amber just keeps looking at me. "No, no. You?" *WHY? YOU STUPID ASS, WHY DID YOU ASK HER THAT?*

Amber's eyes drop to the floor, and she shakes her head slowly. "No. Well, not anymore." She laughs, another unhappy sound, and she puts the book back on the shelf, sliding it back into its place with a decided thud. "More fool me, I guess."

My protective instincts kick in, and I stand up straighter. "Did someone hurt you?"

Amber waves a hand without looking at me. "Nothing I won't survive."

"Amber."

"He was just some loser." She turns to face me, frowning. "I thought when a guy says that he loves you, that he'd mean it. He didn't. So..." It's her turn to trail off now, to shrug, the corners of her mouth tugging a little to show just how much this fucking asshole hurt her.

"I know people," I say, and Amber's face breaks into a smile. "Just saying."

"You gonna get your buddies to beat up a college kid for me?"

"If that's what you want. You just say the word."

Amber laughs softly. "I'll keep that in mind."

"Good." I break the hold her eyes have on mine, and round my desk to sit down. "Now, which books were you wanting? I can't even remember which ones I suggested."

"I think they were down here," Amber says.

"Where?" I look up to see which shelf she's bent down to reach... And freeze.

Amber Pope, my daughter's best friend, a fucking twenty-year-old woman, is bent over, legs slightly apart, her skirt riding up to reveal that she *isn't wearing panties.* And I'm staring at what's right there, not even 9 feet away from me, pink and soft and smooth. I practically punch myself in the groin, willing the bulge that's already springing up to disappear. How can I be staring at...

Wait.

Wait.

"Amber," I say, my voice dropping into a tenor that I haven't used in some fucking time, and not the tone of voice I should use right fucking now.

She straightens, looking over her shoulder at me, her face the picture of innocence.

"Yes, sir?"

Punching myself in the groin isn't fucking enough. Why don't I have a bucket of ice water under my desk?

"Amber, what are you doing?"

"Looking for a book. Why?"

I frown, leaning back in my chair. "A book?"

"Yes, sir." She turns back to the shelf, and leans back

down, bending at the waist, and again her skirt rides up, and again, reveals that sweet, pink pussy. "I'm sure it was right down here."

That wasn't an accident. *That* wasn't a goddamn accident. Amber is bending over in my office and showing herself to me on purpose.

For a moment, I don't know what to do. I know what I *should* do. I'm old enough to be this girl's father, for god's sake. I'm better than the caveman instincts that are kicking in, telling me to go over there and drop to my knees, to taste what's being presented to me. I'm a grown man, I can exercise some self-restraint, and not think about what this girl tastes like, what she feels like, what sounds she'd make when - *No, stop it.*

I slowly get to my feet, staying securely behind the desk, because I need there to be some barrier between us. If there's not... Yeah, I don't need to think about that right now.

"Amber," I say softly. "Honey, I think you should go."

She straightens slowly and puts her hands on the shelf. Her shoulders draw up a little as she takes a deep breath.

"You... don't like me?"

Oh no. No, no, not good. Bad.

"Of course I like you. But-"

"But what?" She turns around to face me, her eyes hooded and sexy. "I'm not your type?"

I grunt out an embarrassed laugh. "God, listen, that is not the problem at all. You're gorgeous. Really. And I am extremely flattered. If I were twenty years younger, you'd absolutely be my type. But-"

"But what?"

"Amber, you're my daughter's best friend." I try to keep my tone even, caught between exasperation and arousal, regretting the decision to get to my feet because I'm sure my jeans aren't doing a good job hiding just what she's done to me. "You're a young woman, you were a kid doing her homework in my office just a few years ago."

"I had a crush on you back then," Amber admits, her hands hidden behind her again. "When I was 17, I used to think... I used to wonder if you were a good kisser."

I rub my forehead and wince. "Listen, you're a beautiful girl, you really are. And if things were different-"

"If I were some girl in a bar that you just met and wasn't friends with your daughter?" She takes a few steps towards my desk. "If I didn't know you and you didn't know me, would you take me home then?"

Her face is so determined, so set with desire, and she's definitely not a girl anymore. She's a woman making her intentions clear, letting me know what she wants, and that she wants me. But it's wrong, so wrong.

"Laurie would kill me," I say pathetically. "I mean, what would you do if one of your friends slept with your dad?"

Amber shrugs. "You're just changing the subject now."

I run my hands through my hair. "Amber, listen, I am too old for you. I am not the kind of guy you should be pursuing. You need to be dating young guys, who you can plan a future with, who-"

"Who fuck me missionary and ask me if I came?" Amber laughs harshly. "Who can't find the clit and get pissed when you point it out to them? Who want head but won't go down on you? *Those* are the guys I should be wasting my time on?"

I cross my arms over my chest and frown. "Is that what this is about? You... want someone with experience?"

"Maybe?" She juts out her chin, pursing those full, glossy lips. "Guys my age have no idea what they're doing.

And they'll say anything to get you into bed, they'll even say they love you. I don't feel safe with them, and I want to know what that feels like. I deserve that, don't I?"

I sigh, my shoulders dropping. "Yes, you do, of course you do. I'm so sorry you've been treated that way. But you have to know, I'm not the answer to that."

"Why not?" A few more steps towards my desk, her gaze never once breaking from my face. "I'm not asking for anything serious. I don't expect that. I just... I want to experience things with someone who'll care for me, who'll make me feel good. And I want to feel safe while I do it."

"I... Look, again, I am flattered. But..." I huff out a breath. "What makes you think I'm going to be so different? That I'm going to be so much better in bed than these guys at college?"

Amber chews on her lip for a second, then gives me a shy smile. "Have you ever had any complaints?"

"That is really not a question to ask a guy," I say with an embarrassed laugh. "We're pretty terrible at self-awareness most of the time."

"I heard Mella talking to my mom one night." Her cheeks flush pink, and her eyes drop from mine. "They were a little tipsy, and Mella was complaining about her latest date, and how bad he'd been in bed." Her eyes drift back up to meet mine, and the desire that's lighting them heats my blood. "She said, 'When am I ever going to meet someone who can fuck half as good as Theo could?'"

Well, now *that* has my ego swelling to a point that should be humiliating. My face is hot and I rub the back of my neck with a strained laugh. "Oh. I see."

"I trust you. I think you're a good man, and a sweet guy, and you're hot, and..." Amber's shoulders jerk in a small shrug. "No one has to know. Laurie included. Nothing has to change."

"I think sex can change a lot, don't you?"

"Not if we don't let it." Amber's mouth twitches into a soft smile. "The fact you're talking this in circles tells me you're thinking about it."

"Listen, a pretty girl in my office with no panties on, yeah, that's kind of tempting."

"Then just... Give in." She shrugs with a smile. "It's just sex. Just two people, who want to spend a weekend together, and then we go back to our lives Monday morning."

I regard her face with a heavy breath. This is wrong Her father would fucking murder me if he ever found out I'd touched his daughter. I've played golf with him, I've drunk beers in this man's yard while our kids danced to too-loud music. We've commiserated about our kids heading to college. We've sworn that any man who hurts our little girls would fucking pay.

And now I'm looking at Amber, considering just how bad it would be to peel those clothes off her and spend the weekend showing her what a man of my age, with my experience, can do.

Fuck it.

"We don't tell anyone," I say, and Amber's mouth shifts as she suppresses a smile. "This is just about us."

"Yes." She nods.

"If I make you uncomfortable, or anything hurts, anything at all, you tell me to stop, OK?" I raise my eyebrows. "Promise?"

"Yes, of course."

Tell her to leave and that this is a mistake. What are you doing? But it's too late. I'm no longer the jovial dad, I'm a man, and she's a woman, and we're negotiating terms for how this weekend in bed is going to go. It's thrilling in a way that should have me hanging my head in shame.

"Are you on birth control?" I ask, and I hate the spark of joy that springs up when she nods Yes. "That's good, but I'm still going to wear a condom, of course." I do some crazy mental gymnastics in that split second, thinking where I even have condoms and if they're still in date, because it's been a good while since I needed one.

"You don't have to," Amber says, and the uncertainty in her face tells me exactly what these assholes at college have been doing to her. "I've been tested, and-"

"Honey, listen to me." I round the desk, so we're only a few feet apart. I want to touch her and take her in my arms, but we need to get this all out first. "I've been tested too, but that's not the point. Sex without a condom feels great, but it feels good with one too. And your health is what's important to me. I will not pressure you or tell you they don't fit me, or any other shit a guy has said to you to manipulate you into doing what he wanted."

She smiles softly, her face so filled with relief and trust that I'm determined to get this guy's name before the weekend is done and see if I can't make his life a living hell.

"I knew you'd be good to me," she says.

You have no idea how good I can be to you. My reason is disgusted with me. But we're past all of that now. It's happening, and where a few minutes ago I was hesitating, now I want it, I want her, and I want this weekend to show her how a man should treat her. What's the worst that could happen?

"Now," I say, moving closer to her, almost closing the distance between us, and sweep her hair over her shoulder. "I'd really, really like to kiss you."

She licks her lips, with the barest shiver of a nod. "OK."

I move to take off my glasses, and she reaches up to stop me, shaking her head. "Leave them on. Please."

I lower my mouth to hers with a smile. Her breath catches just a little as my lips brush against hers, all that heat and promise washing over me. Her eyes are still open, looking into mine, as though she's trying to peer deep enough to see into my soul.

My other hand trails along her jaw, my fingers threading into her hair, so I can hold her head as I kiss her for the first time. *My fucking god.* The feeling when we're finally against each other, finally kissing, her full lips opening for my tongue, is sheer paradise. She tastes fresh and sweet, a soft moan quivering in her throat. This is impulsive, and stupid. I couldn't even take an hour to think about it?

Then she wraps her arms around my waist, her hands on my back, and the voice that was screaming at me that this is wrong shuts the hell up.

Amber presses into me, her kiss becoming more urgent, as though she's trying to rush, to move faster, but I'm going to take my time with her. I'm not going to regret this right now. I can beat myself up for being a dirty old man later.

"I was right," she says with a small smile when we part, her eyes still closed. "You are a good kisser."

"I'm glad I lived up to the fantasy," I say, trailing kisses along her jaw, down to her neck. "And you're a pretty good kisser yourself."

"Oh yeah?" She gasps a little as my lips brush a spot, just behind her ear, and she shivers.

"I'll remember that for later," I say with a chuckle. "Now, go and sit on my desk."

She blinks up at me, her lips so plump and pretty, kiss-stung and red. "*On* your desk?"

"Yes, honey." I trace my thumb along her lower lip. "I want to see what you were showing me, but this time I want to see it up close."

Her cheeks flush bright red, but she nods with a small smile and takes a step back, peeling her sweater off and dropping it to the ground. She's wearing a white button-down underneath, undone just far enough for me to see the barest glimpse of the red lace of her bra. When her hands move to undo the rest of the buttons, I reach out and still her movements.

"I'd really like to do that."

She licks her lips and nods, then does as I say, and walks over to the desk, perching on the edge, one leg demurely crossed over the other. She watches me curiously as I sit down, her eyes following my hand as I reach to caress the bare skin that's visible between the hemline of her skirt and those adorable thigh-high socks.

Her breathing picks up at the touch of my hand, her thighs clenching together. I look up at her questioningly.

"Is this alright?"

She nods quickly.

"You don't have to be nervous." I take off my glasses. "If you don't want to do anything, we stop immediately. You just say the word."

"I know," she breathes, and puts her hand over mine. "I trust you."

"Thank you. Now, I want you to put your heels on the desk for me," I say in a low voice, and her eyes widen a little. "I'd like you nice and open for what I'm going to do."

"Are you... Are you going to go down on me?"

I can't help but raise an eyebrow. "No one ever has before?"

She shakes her head, and I swear my disappointment in the men of the world is palpable.

"Do you actually like it?" She asks shyly.

I chuckle, running my hands down her legs. "Are you kidding? I love it."

"Really?"

"Yes, really. Now..." I run my hands under the hem of her skirt, and she lets out a sweet little gasp. "Are you going to put your heels up on the desk so I can see your pussy?"

Her cheeks flush a deeper shade of pink, and she slowly uncrosses her legs, raising them and planting her heels against the edge of the desk. I lean back to see, and sure enough, the sight she presented to me from across my office is even prettier up close. She's wetter now, turned on and swollen, glistening sinfully in the afternoon light. I exhale through lightly gritted teeth, palming my dick through my jeans, trying to relieve something of the ache and the need that's overcoming me. Because I know I need to slow down and focus on my girl, and make her feel good before I even think of doing anything about myself.

"Goddamn," I murmur, and run my hands down her thighs. "You're beautiful."

She giggles softly, and I know being this open and vulnerable is probably a lot for her. I take off my sweater, and her face is alight with surprised delight.

"You have tattoos?"

I look down at my chest and shrug. "Sure do."

"I like them."

"I'll let you take a closer look later." I return my attention to her, to that delicious cunt that's perched right here on my desk, and I ask myself how I got this fucking lucky.

Touching her feels like crashing right through an electric fence, past all the signs that say *Danger! Go Back!*

The shiver that goes through her as my finger strays over her clit sets my nerves on fire. Her head falls back as I rub her in slow circles, and she moans. I push a finger inside her gently, not wanting to hurt her. She's tight and hot, and she claps a hand over her mouth as I stroke inside her.

"You don't have to be quiet here," I say to her, and her hand drops from her mouth. "You can scream as loud as you want, honey." I add a second finger, and I have to clench my jaw hard to calm myself down, because fucking christ almighty, she feels so good.

As my fingers continue to work her, I lower my mouth to her soft, pink skin. I close my mouth over her clit, and suck. She bucks, crying out, a hand shooting through my hair and grabbing hard. It doesn't hurt, not a bit, it feels fucking amazing, and the hot, wet pussy right in my face would be distraction enough. *Holy shit.* I forgot how much I really do love eating a woman out. I can't help but groan as I swirl my tongue around her clit, my fingers gently working inside her, pressing against her g-spot.

"Theo," she murmurs, her fingers sprawling and clutching at my hair. "*Oh*, oh my *god.*"

I withdraw my fingers from her, licking her off them, then push them back inside, massaging her clit with my tongue. She tastes so sweet, so damn good, her juices soaking the beard I'd allowed to grow over the past couple weeks of being too busy to shave. I could douse myself in this smell, this heat, cover myself in her, and be fucking happy.

How did I even end up here? I don't care, I shouldn't care, and I don't even know how I would ever explain to anyone that I was here, in my damn office on a fall afternoon, bringing a college student to orgasm with my mouth.

Her thighs shake, her breath hitching, and I feverishly think where my damn condoms are, because I need to be inside her as soon as she comes. They're upstairs, I know they are, *fuck why couldn't I be prepared for this??* I force myself to forget about that, and focus on Amber, on her moans and cries. Her cunt is clenching my fingers now, and then my tongue finds a spot that has her back arching, her body tense as it teeters right on the brink of release.

"Don't stop! Don't stop!" She cries.

There isn't a possible world where I'd stop. I lick and suck like a man starved, and with a loud moan, Amber comes on my desk, her fingers sinking into my hair, her body shaking and her breath escaping her in short, hard gasps.

"Oh my god," she moans. "Oh, oh my fucking god."

I lick until she can't stand it, until the clench of her thighs tells me she's too sensitive to take anymore. I kiss her thighs, opening my jeans and releasing my dick, fisting myself with a groan.

"Fuck, I need to be inside you," I mutter against her skin.

"Just do it," she says, her head still thrown back. "Please, just, I don't care, just do it."

That would be irresponsible. I know it. She's not in her right mind, and I know better than to do something like that.

"I'm not fucking you without a condom." I rise to my feet and she rolls her head on her shoulders back around to look at me. "Believe me, I really fucking want to. But I won't do that."

"Please, Theo, I want to know what you feel like." She whimpers as my hand brushes over the nipple peaking through her shirt. "Just... just the tip, please? You don't have to come inside me, just... Please? Then we can go upstairs."

This is a bad idea. It's a really fucking bad idea. I'm leaking pre-cum everywhere, my cock slick with arousal and need. With a frustrated moan, Amber reaches down to wrap her hand around me, pushing mine out of the way, and her eyes fly open.

"Oh, my god." She looks down between us at my throbbing cock, pumping me gently, and I clench my jaw, my fingers digging into the hardwood of the desk to stop myself from coming. "You're... You're huge."

My ego swells in a way it shouldn't. I know I'm well-endowed. It was something plenty of my sexual partners liked about me. Mella (*why the fuck am I thinking about my ex right now??*) used to compare it to being fucked by a wine bottle. I know I'm big. But to be met with awe like this, it inflates my brain and my stupid masculine sense of self, and now I really want to fuck this girl without a condom, feel her tight pussy stretch around me and watch her eyes roll back in her head as she clenches me and I pump her full of cum.

I really am a fucking caveman.

"Just the tip," I grit out, and move closer, letting her guide me. "Then we stop, and I'm going to take you upstairs, and fuck you properly."

She keeps her eyes locked on where the blunt head of my dick is pressing to her entrance. If she weren't this turned on, if I hadn't made her come with my tongue first, this would be a fight. I've had to go slow before, had partners have to breathe through it as I pushed inside them. Lube, always plenty of lube. But Amber is soaked, and just running my head through her heat is enough to tell me this is a terrible idea. I'm going to come inside this girl in an instant.

She's so slippery that when I breach her, and slip the head of my cock inside her, just a tiny jerk of my hips has me sinking deeper than I was supposed to. She looks up at me, somewhere between alarm and sheer delight.

"Just like that," she says, her eyelids fluttering. "Oh god, just... stay like that for a second."

I'm leaning over her, trying to maintain control, and I lean in to kiss her, to taste her sweet tongue again as just a few inches of my cock rest inside her. I haven't had unprotected sex in forever, and holy fuck, it feels too good.

Amber shifts her hips, and I groan into her mouth.

"Honey, if you do that again, I'm going to come inside you," I say with a strained laugh. "You feel too fucking good to be doing that."

"You can," she murmurs, and she lifts her hips a little to try and take in more of me. "Just fuck me. Please."

"Amber." I pull out of her and am met with a frustrated whimper. I lean my forehead against hers, breathing hard. "I need to take you upstairs right now."

———

I must have been a Catholic in a past life. I was probably extremely devout, and into flagellation and self-denial. There is no other reason I can think of for me to delay fucking Amber further by taking her upstairs and undressing her slowly. First, the skirt. That doesn't take much, but somehow, I make even that last, working it down over her hips and her peachy, round ass, to drop to the floor.

She's a vision in that loose button-down and the socks. Like something out of a dirty magazine. I want a picture of her, just as she is now, illuminated in sunlight, glossy hair tossed over her shoulder, naked thighs and bedroom eyes.

Fuck, my girl is beautiful.

I undo the buttons next, one by one, knowing that the tits waiting for me are perfect. And god, they are. She's wearing a slinky little bra, red and lacy, her nipples visible, hard and peaked. I suck one into my mouth, lace and all, before the shirt is all the way undone, and Amber gasps. My tongue probes the lace, the sensation of hot skin through the resistance of fabric making us both moan.

The button-down lands on the floor, and I peel the bra down her shoulders, reaching around to unclip the two little hooks. Then she's there, like a goddess, like an angel of sin and temptation, in the middle of my bright bedroom, in nothing but thigh-high white socks. Her skin is still glowing golden from the summer sun, her breasts full and round, crowned with tan nipples.

"You're so fucking beautiful," I say to her, pulling her against my naked chest and bringing my mouth down on hers. It's a hungry kiss this time, not slow and sensual, but raw and bruising, filled with need.

Her body is feverish, with the orgasm that just coursed through her a few minutes ago, with the sunshine that streams in through the window, with the heat that's seeping from my body to hers. She lifts her arms, wrapping them around my neck, and she shrieks against my mouth as I put my hands under her ass and lift her up.

"You're so strong," she murmurs, and pinches my lower lip between her teeth. "You could probably fuck me against the wall if you wanted to, huh?"

"Maybe later," I say with a grin, walking her over to my

bed and laying her down on her back. "Right now, I want to take things slow with you. I don't want to hurt you."

She bites her lip as she watches me slip off my jeans, lifting herself up on her elbows. When I free my dick from my boxer briefs, her eyes widen again, and she releases her lip from her teeth.

"Have... have you ever had any problems with, like, sex?"

I give her a smile and shake my head. "You only have problems if you don't care about your partner."

"Not a problem for a guy like you, I guess?" She gives me a grin, tossing her hair, and, fucking christ, this girl sprawled out with her legs open and her perfect tits, she's a dream.

"Not at all." I go to the drawer and rifle around for a second to find the condoms, tearing open a packet and throwing it to the ground before rolling the condom down over my length. I inhale deeply through my nose, because I'm so sensitive now even touching myself has me biting back a groan. Amber sits up quickly, reaching out for me.

"Are you OK?"

"Honey, I am fine," I say with a smile. "I just got so turned on eating you on my desk that I nearly came in my pants."

She covers a giggle with her hand. "You liked it that much?"

With the condom now on, I lean over her on the bed, kissing my way along her collarbone, up her throat, and she lies back with a sigh.

"I liked it that much," I say, my mouth moving over her chest. "You feel incredible. You taste so good. I could stay down there forever." I take one of her nipples into my mouth, and she tenses with a whimper. The tip of my cock brushes her leg, and the sensation has me sucking her nipple hard, almost reflexively, and she cries out.

"Sorry." I release her plump breast, and look up at her. "Did I hurt you?"

She shakes her head. "No, not at all. It felt... It felt good."

"Good." I want to explore her body more, I want to spend hours tracing my tongue over all of her golden glowing skin, but I know if I don't get inside her right now, if I delay any further, it'll be over embarrassingly fast.

Her thighs fall open for me, allowing me to settle between them, her big brown eyes gazing up at me. I stay with her, with that open, trusting look, as I guide the tip of my cock through her slickness.

"You're so wet," I murmur. "You're so wet and ready for me, aren't you?"

"Yes," she gasps. "Please, I want to feel you."

I gently nudge myself against her entrance, and at this angle, she feels tighter than when she was splayed and open on my desk.

"Breathe for me, honey," I tell her softly, and she exhales a shaky breath as I slip inside her, just the first inch. Holy hell, it's almost a fight. Sweat breaks out on the back of my neck with the strain of holding back. As wet as she is, I still have to take it slow, I can't just plunge inside her and fuck her hard.

She gasps as she stretches, another shaky breath passing her lips.

"I'm OK," she says quickly, and she brings her hands up to my face, to cradle it gently as she presses her forehead to mine. I look into this face, this beautiful face, and I can't believe my cock is inside her, inside *her*.

"Am I hurting you?

She shakes her head. "No, I want more."

I sink in a little further, and her back arches in a jolt, pressing her tits against my chest.

"Don't stop," she hisses, slinging her legs around my hips.

"We're taking it slow, honey." *Like fuck we are.* The feeling of her clenched around me is already stirring that heat and pressure in my groin. I'm more than halfway inside her when her brow pinches, and she sucks in a breath through her gritted teeth. "Does that hurt?"

She laughs softly. "No, you're just... You're right against my g-spot. I've never..." She shakes her head, brushing her lips against mine. "Keep going. It feels so good."

Finally, after more breathing, more angling of her hips to open her sweet pussy right up for me, I'm inside her, buried to the damn hilt, and I release a soft groan against her lips.

"Fuck," I murmur, my heart hammering at my chest. "Holy *fuck*." Even with the condom, I can feel her heat, and the caveman inside me wishes I weren't so damn gallant so I could just tear it off and feel her completely. But I stay like that for a moment, kissing her mouth, along her jaw, the soft place behind her ear that has her shivering. "Oh my god, Amber, you feel too fucking good."

She rocks her hips in response, wordlessly urging me to move, which I do, sliding out and back in slowly, earning me a moan, her hands grasping my face tighter.

"You're shaking."

"I'm alright. Just... holding back."

"Don't," she says, shaking her head. "Please, just fuck me. I want to feel you come now."

Oh god, those words are almost enough to have me spilling immediately.

I begin to move, and that's a whole other fight in itself. I'm caught between checking the movements and tension in her body for any hint of pain, and my aching need for release, to fuck her and come inside her. But if I was looking for any sign of pain, there isn't one. As hard as I have to push to get inside her, to sink right down, down into those sweet, heavenly depths of her body, she does nothing but moan, and dig her nails into my back.

She's so wet, so perfectly wet and open, and she leans up to kiss me slowly.

"Oh, Theo," she murmurs, her back bowing away from the bed, but gently this time, her body moving in time with me.

"Is that good, honey?" I ask, kissing and nibbling along her jaw.

She nods eagerly, her eyes closed now. "More." She locks her legs around my waist, tipping her hips back, and the angle has me groaning loudly into the crook of her neck.

"Oh shit," I mutter, panting. I want to pound myself into her, but I can't, not like this, I know I'll hurt her if I do. "Honey, we need to change positions."

"Why?" Her eyes fly open with alarm. "Am I hurting you?"

I kiss her lips and shake my head. "No, but I want to do this harder, and I don't want to hurt you."

I sit up on my knees, taking her legs and planting her feet against my stomach. She's panting, watching curiously, her eyebrows raised. She flexes her toes along the hard ridge of my muscles, and she bites her lip. The fact she likes my body, that she thinks it's hot, even, does things to me it shouldn't. Another inflating ego boost, swelling my head and every other fucking thing about me.

"If it goes too deep, push back, OK?" I ask, waiting for her to nod, which she does.

I look down at her pussy, stretched and pink and perfect. I pull all the way out, and she makes a small, displeased whimper at the emptiness, but I did this just so I could watch her take me again. Watching her stretch for me, it's like being drugged. My dick almost looks grotesque, impaling her like this, raw and red, angry and aching with the need for release. And there, planted firmly inside her soft, slick skin, it's like her pussy was made for me.

Slow down, old man. This isn't like that. Show the girl a good time.

I yank myself out of my thoughts, and look back up at her face. Her lower lip is quivering, and she moans as my thumb circles her clit.

"Does that feel good for you, honey?" I thrust my hips gently.

"Yes, oh god, yes." Her back arches off the bed. "Harder."

My hand digs into her thigh as I fuck her harder, not wanting to let go too much, not wanting to hurt her and scare her after what those other assholes have done to her, but it's a fight.

She massages her breasts, pinching her nipples between her fingers, and I am definitely going to watch this girl masturbate later, because seeing her play with her own tits is one of the hottest things I've ever seen.

I feel her orgasm before her moans betray it, a sharp pulse making my thrusts almost impossible. Then she's crying out, saying my name, like she's begging for something, *Theo, Theo,* and I answer with a grunt, heat flashing through my spine.

"Jesus, honey. Oh, my god." I'm going to come. While

Amber's pussy is still fluttering around my cock, I throw my head back, and my orgasm collides with hers, shattering through me in waves of heat. It's now, now in this moment that I wish more than ever I wasn't such a fucking gentleman, because I want to feel my heat meet hers, I want to pump her quivering pussy full of me, I want to see it spill out when I pull out of her, not have it coating my cock inside the sheath of the condom.

But fuck, it feels good anyway.

I look down at her, at Amber, at this perfect angel spread out on my bed, her arms thrown out to her sides, her hair a wild, copper tangle. Her lips are full, puffing out one breath after another. Her eyes meet mine, and she smiles. Wide and satisfied.

"Oh my god," she murmurs, pressing a hand to her eyes. "Fuck. That was incredible."

"Yes, it was." I gently lift one of her feet from my stomach, kissing her ankle before placing it on the bed, repeating the action with her other foot. "You feel, I mean… Jesus. You're amazing."

She props herself up on her elbows, looking down to where we're joined. "I've never felt so… filled. I don't know, it was… Like there was nothing but you." She watches with almost virginal fascination as I withdraw from her, hissing in a breath when I'm all the way out.

My embarrassingly large load of cum fills the tip of the condom, and she giggles.

"Is there such a thing as a cum fetish?" She asks. "Because if there is, I think I have one."

"Oh, yeah?"

"Mhmm." She lifts her eyes to mine. "All I kept thinking was how I wanted you to come inside me." She wrinkles her nose, her cheeks flushing an even deeper shade of pink. "That's weird, right?"

"Not at all, honey." I lean down and give her a soft kiss, before climbing off the bed to deal with the condom in the bathroom.

In the mirror, I look into the face of the dirty old man who just fucked his daughter's best friend. I don't even look guilty. I look fucking pleased with myself. I just came inside the body of a twenty-year-old, and there's not even a shred of guilt on my face.

This is wrong. It's so, so wrong.

Cleaned up, I head back to the bed, throwing myself down beside Amber, who immediately snuggles up under my arm and lays her head on my chest. She sighs happily, and I stroke my fingers over her silky copper hair, which shines red in the fading late afternoon light.

"That was fun," she says, her fingers making tiny circles on my chest.

"Yes, it was. It was just over way too fast for my liking."

She looks up at me with a slow smile, her brown eyes sparkling. "Oh, yeah?"

"Yeah." I stroke a finger along her jaw, then run my thumb over her lips. "I'd love to spend hours doing that."

"Well, I'm yours till Monday." She runs a hand down my stomach, towards my hip, and I tense, which makes her giggle. "You have all weekend to do just what you want to me."

"Mmm, but what about what you want?"

She rests her chin on my chest, pursing her lips as she thinks. "I don't know, I guess there's a few things I always wanted to try."

"Such as?" I tuck a strand of hair behind her ear, still

marvelling at how beautiful she is, and that she's here naked, in my bed.

She rolls her eyes. "It probably sounds stupid to a worldly man like you. But, I don't know, like... being bent over?"

I frown at her. "Bent over? Asin being fucked from behind?" When she nods, I can't help but laugh. "Oh my god, what are these young men doing these days?"

"Obsessing over anal sex and cumshots," Amber says with a grimace. "It's gross."

"You don't like anal?"

She shakes her head adamantly. "No. It's not my thing. It hurts, and it feels so unsexy, I never want to try it again." She lifts her head to look down at my dick resting against my thigh. "Especially not with that thing."

I chuckle, stroking the back of my fingers down her bare shoulder. "It's not a requirement, I promise. We do what you want. But what else besides doggy style would you like to try?"

She puts her chin back on my chest, tapping her fingers pensively against my skin. "I guess... I'd like to try being on top?" She eyes me with a shy laugh. "I probably sound so unadventurous to you right now. I just... I haven't had that much experience."

"Do you watch porn?"

She nods after a beat, her cheeks flaming yet again. "I have. To see what I like, what I, y'know, react to?"

I surprise myself, because this conversation has me already getting hard again as I imagine Amber in her bed all alone, playing with herself while she watches porn on her phone.

"And what do you react to, honey?"

She sits up, pushing her hair over her shoulder and

biting her lip. "I... I like those, you know, free use videos? Where he just does what he wants when he wants? I find that kind of hot."

"I think that is pretty hot." I reach out to cup her breast, running a thumb over her nipple, and she sucks in a quick breath. "You like that kind of thing? Being used?"

The smile drops, and she sighs. "I... I've never been with someone where I felt comfortable doing something like that. I just, I guess I've never trusted someone like that, and for those things you need a lot of trust."

"That's very true, you do."

She scoffs and looks over her shoulder to gaze at the sunset. "All these young guys, talking big about being doms and all that shit, it's just an excuse to treat a woman like a fucking fleshlight."

I don't know what to say for a moment, and I worry about how much pain there is behind those words. But when I sit up beside her, she turns to me with a smile.

"That's why I wanted you." She puts her arms around my neck, and I pull her on top of me. "I knew I could trust you. You're a good guy. You'll treat me right, make me feel special. And I don't have to go back to college all inexperienced."

"I'm setting the standard for you, am I?"

She giggles, then kisses me, a slow, heated kiss, that has my blood rising again. The softness of her tongue, her plump lips - this girl is heaven. Heaven, and she's on my lap, grinding her sweet needy pussy against my cock until I'm hard again.

And she's mine til Monday.

I'm going to make every second count.

2

FRIDAY NIGHT

Not bad for a man of your age.

The self-satisfied thought circles my orgasm-addled brain as I try to catch my breath. Amber's body is nestled against mine, my cock still buried inside her. Night has come and the sky is pitch black, and we've fucked three times since that first time. Once, on the way to the shower - which we still haven't taken. Once with Amber bent over the edge of my bed, her nails almost tearing holes into my sheets as she screamed for me. And now, her back to my chest, our legs entangled, my arms locked around her as I slowly, achingly worked her back to another orgasm.

Fucking christ, what a way to spend a Friday night.

My phone buzzed a few times, probably Laurie telling me about the progression of their trip, and I feel a pang of guilt. If she knew what I was doing right now, *who* I was doing right now...

"Theo," Amber murmurs, crashing through my thoughts and drawing me back into the moment.

"Yes, honey?" I nuzzle into her hair, breathing in the

scent of sugar and berries that clings to her hair, like sweet cotton candy.

"I'm starving."

I laugh into the crook of her neck, pressing a kiss to her shoulder. "So am I." I pull out of her, another condom filled with my release, and I know it'll mean a trip to the store before tomorrow is out because my supply is depleting fast. Never in my life could I have prepared for a weekend long fuck-fest with a woman less than half my age.

Dirty old man.

I tell my inner judgmental old asshole to shut the fuck up.

"What are you hungry for?" I ask as I head to the bathroom, a well-worn path by now.

"I could kill for some noodles," she calls back, and when I emerge from the bathroom she's wearing one of my t-shirts and a pair of my boxers. She's winding her hair up on the top of her head, and she looks so perfect, here in my bedroom. She gives me a smile, her eyes wandering over my naked body. "I hope you don't mind, I helped myself to your clothes. I'll have to go get mine tomorrow."

"You look so damn good." I cross the room to snatch her up in my arms, and she giggles as I kiss her neck. "Who knew a woman wearing my underwear could be such an aphrodisiac?"

"See? I told you that you were exaggerating about your age. Getting horny again already." She turns her head to kiss my mouth and then rubs her face against my beard. "Now, go order me noodles or I'll be grumpy."

I reluctantly let her go, crossing the room to pull some sweatpants from the wardrobe. "Well, we cannot have a grumpy Amber, can we?"

"No, we cannot."

The slow smile she gives me, artfully securing her hair with a flick of her hands and no hair tie, the way her tits look under the fabric of my shirt - the tits that were just in my mouth, in my face, pressed to my sheets - all of it, combines into something within me that's... dangerous.

She tilts her head, her brows pinching together for a second, and I realise I'm staring.

"Noodles, right?" I take my phone from the nightstand, ignoring the notifications from Laurie, from Mella, from my buddies at the gym. "Madame Wong's delivers, that alright with you?"

"Sure. Chicken chow mein, please!" She struts out of the bedroom, and I hear her footsteps pad down the stairs. "And crab rangoon!"

I smile and shake my head, opening the menu and selecting her noodles, her crab rangoon, and deciding against my usual order of Kung Pao chicken, picking beef and broccoli instead. *Am I trying to impress a girl with my healthier food choices?* I really am an old fool.

I follow her downstairs, and into the kitchen, where she's perched on the granite countertop, enormous glass of water in her hand, long legs swinging back and forth. She grins at me as I lean against the counter beside her, and she hands me the glass of water.

"So," she says, her eyebrows raised.

"So." I take a long, quenching gulp of water.

"Any regrets?"

I choke on the water that's flowing down my throat, and she laughs as I give her a bewildered look.

"Hitting me with the hard questions, huh?" I chide, wiping my mouth with the back of my hand.

"Just asking." She plucks the glass from my hand, placing it on the counter beside us, and pulls me towards her, wrapping her legs around my waist. "Because I don't have any."

I run my hands over her head, bringing them to rest at the base of her neck, gazing down into her big, warm eyes. "Neither do I." I kiss her forehead, the tip of her nose, the corner of her mouth. "I hope I didn't hurt you."

"Not at all." She nuzzles against my chest, head tucked under my chin. "I can't wait to do it again."

I laugh softly. "Well, the food will take a little while. But..." I pull back from her and cradle her face in my hands. "The condoms are all the way upstairs, so." I shrug, and Amber giggles.

"Well, you could just eat me out again instead?"

She shrieks as I yank down the boxer briefs she's wearing and sink to my knees.

"Theo, oh my god!" She laughs, but that dissolves quickly into moaning as I bring my mouth down to her pussy, swirling my tongue inside her. "I was - Oh god, I was joking!"

I wasn't.

The damn phone rings.

It's Laurie's ringtone. She must be frantic. Or maybe something happened? *Shit.* I'm here fucking her best friend, and maybe they had an accident.

I stop and look up at Amber with a sigh.

"I should take this, it's Laurie."

She nods, tucking a loose strand of hair behind her ear. She licks her lips, clasping her thighs together as I get to my feet and swipe my phone to answer Laurie's call.

"Hey, peanut!" God, I may not have looked guilty, but I sound it now. "You all good?"

"Where were you?" Laurie's exasperated tone sounds down the line. "I've sent you a million snaps."

"Sorry, I... I went to the gym and got sidetracked." My eyes flash to Amber, who's avoiding my gaze. "Anyway, how was the drive? Grandma and Grandpa OK?"

"Yeah, they're great. We're just getting dinner." She pauses, noise and commotion and the jangle of keys in the background. "Is something wrong?"

"Nope, everything here is just fine, why?"

"You just... sound weird." Laurie mutters something to someone beside her that sounds like *Yeah he's fine*, and I realise now that it's been hours since they left and no one has been able to reach me. "You just scared me, is all."

"Oh, peanut, I'm sorry. I'm fine, I promise. Just getting in those gym hours, you know?"

"Yeah yeah, you and the gym." The worry lifts from her voice, and she laughs. "I know how you can get."

"You sure do."

"Is Amber home?"

My heart drops into my fucking feet. How could she know? Did someone see Amber come here and realise she never went home? *Fuck. Bad. Very bad.*

"I-I have no idea. Why? Is Amber meant to be home?"

Amber's head shoots up at the mention of her name, and she shakes her head.

"Yeah, she said she'd be home today, but I haven't been able to reach her all afternoon. I'm just worried."

My heart is still thumping at the base of my stomach, having not made it all the way back to where it's meant to be after the mention of Amber's name. I take a deep breath and steady myself, trying to sound bright and normal, fucking *normal*.

"Listen, I'll, uh, I'll go by her house on my way back from the gym and make sure her car is there. She probably just went right to bed after the drive."

"Yeah, you're probably right." Laurie mutters, *I'm coming,* and sighs. "I gotta go. Mom's new boyfriend is taking us out." Her voice drops a little, and I can't help but wonder if the new boyfriend hasn't impressed as much as Mella was hoping.

"Well, you have fun!" Thank fuck my voice doesn't crack with the enthusiasm I put into that statement.

"Love you, Dad!"

"Love you, peanut!"

She's gone, and I turn back to face Amber, whose face has blanched a little.

"Laurie's looking for you," I say, putting my phone down on the counter and exhaling heavily. "She was freaking out because she couldn't get a hold of either of us."

"She didn't think we're together though, right?"

"No, no, she... she bought it." I chew on my lip, rubbing the back of my neck. Guilt sinks into my stomach. The way we both just panicked should shake some sense into me. We know this is wrong. We know she should go home. What's done is done and we can't take that back, that's bad enough. But it doesn't have to go any further.

But when I look back up at Amber, whose face has some colour in it again as she relaxes, all I can think of is watching her as she comes, the way she moans my name, and I'm damned to hell. I'm not going to let her go, not when she's mine for the next two days.

"I'll write her quick," Amber says, then smacks her hand into her forehead. "I left my phone at home."

"It's fine, I'll tell her I checked in on you and that your car was there. We'll go get your phone later." *When it's really, really dark and no one can see us go to your house together.*

Amber nods, and climbs down from the counter.

"Sounds good." She stands in front of me, smiling and giving me a coy look of satisfaction. "Feels like we're doing something really naughty, doesn't it?"

"Extremely naughty." I back her against the counter, caging her in with my arms. "Very, very, *very* bad."

"Good thing no one will ever know, huh?"

"Mmmm." I run a hand under the white shirt, catching her nipple between my fingers, and she gasps. "It'll be our dirty little secret." I pinch her nipple hard, and her eyes slam shut, a moan escaping her lips. "Our dirty secret that I licked your pussy on my desk, and here in the kitchen."

I don't know what's wrong with me, but the thrill of almost being caught, of just thinking we'd almost been caught, lights my veins on fire. I spin Amber around, pressing her down to the counter so she's bent and almost straining on her tiptoes.

I spear two fingers inside her, and her head snaps up.

"Theo," she says in that tone, that pleading, begging tone I want to imprint on my brain.

"Is that good, honey?"

"Y-yes." She chokes out another moan, her toes curling against the floor.

"Such a pretty pussy." I start in on her clit now, massaging with my thumb as my two fingers continue to stroke inside her. "So wet. You're hungry for my cock again, aren't you?"

She nods wordlessly, fingers clawed against the granite.

"You want it in your mouth?"

She sucks in a breath, and suddenly I have an image in my head that almost has me coming in my damn sweats. Amber, on her knees in just my shirt, plump lips wrapped around my cock, her hands between her legs, getting herself off as I fuck her throat.

Who the fuck am I? Sure, I've enjoyed being rough with partners in the past. I like being dominant. I have kinks. I even have a slightly adventurous sexual history if you want to put it that way. But this? With *her*? Maybe I'm pushing a little too hard.

But she makes my heart race when she nods her pretty head, *Yes*. Her hair's come loose, hanging down by her cheek, and it catches in her breath as she puffs out the word. "Yes. I want to suck your cock. Please."

I slide my fingers out of her, putting them in my mouth to taste her sweetness, and she turns around to face me, her eyes staying on mine as she drops to her knees.

"No hands, pretty girl," I say, winding her hair around my fist. "Just your mouth. Your hands are for you. I want you to fuck your hand, and make yourself come."

Her eyes are alight with desire, warm and deep, and she hooks her hands into my waistband to free my throbbing dick from my sweats. She runs her hand up my stomach, over my abs, wrapping the other around the base of my cock.

She licks the tip, drawing her tongue into her mouth and tasting the pre-cum that's leaking already. She opens her mouth again, laying the tip of my cock on her hot tongue, and removes her hand from me. As her lips close around me, she moans, her fingers hidden by the hem of the t-shirt, but I know she's touching herself.

My brain short-circuits, because it's so much, all of it - watching her touch herself, feeling her mouth around my dick, barely fitting me, barely taking any of me, and I really am a bad man, because that's what makes it so *good*. She's choking lightly, tears pearling at the corners of her eyes, but she pushes and sucks, her tongue swirling over the tip. Her lips vibrate with every moan and gasp that's cut off by my dick, and her hands move faster.

"Fuck, yes," I mutter, gripping her hair, not trying to thrust or force her head down, but wanting to be all the way down her tight throat. I want to lay her down on the table and hang her head off the edge, fucking her throat like that, watching me fill her and choke the air from her.

Who the fuck are you?

I loosen my grip on her hair, suddenly worried I'm scaring her, because I'm a fucking animal. But she protests, pushing more of me into her mouth, and I grit my teeth so hard I know I'm going to knock one out. *Jesus fuck.*

"Amber, fuck. Yeah, just like that." I groan loudly, and now I can't help the reflexive jerk of my hips. "Don't stop, fuck, don't stop."

She inhales sharply through her nostrils, and then a long, keening moan vibrates in her throat, her hands slowing as she rocks her hips. She came. My fucking god, she came here on the floor in my house, sucking my cock.

I shove her head down onto me, and then I'm pumping into her mouth, stream after stream of my release flooding her throat. She chokes, her hands braced against my thighs, her head bobbing lightly, pressure around my tip as she swallows.

I sag, my hand in her hair relaxing.

"Show me," I gasp. "Show me, pretty girl."

She releases me, gasping for air, then looks up at me, eyes hooded, and sticks out her tongue. Her tongue coated in the glistening white of my cum.

"Now, swallow." I say, and she smiles deviously as she

does just that. I huff out a laugh, stroking my thumb over her lips. "You're a fucking dream, honey."

I help her up from the floor, and she wraps her arms around me, laying her body against me as I cup her bare ass with my hands. She doesn't say anything, just stays there, breathing heavy against my chest.

I tell her how beautiful she is, how well she did, and she sighs happily.

This is bliss.

Danger. Danger. Go back.

I ignore the voice.

"I hope I didn't scare you."

She pulls back from me with a frown. "Scare me?"

"Yeah, that I was too rough or something."

She shakes her head. "No, not at all. I liked it. I like... I mean, I think I like it like that. A little rough. Having my hair pulled felt good too." Her frown deepens for a second. "But no choking."

"You don't like that?"

"No." She shakes her head again, and her eyes dart from mine. "I hate it. No hands around the neck."

"Of course, honey." The worry from before comes back, and I wonder again what this guy did to her.

The doorbell announces the arrival of our food, and if she had been consumed by dark memories before, all that seems to be gone as she settles down at the table with me. We eat and laugh and joke, and it's easy. It's nice. She's funny, and witty. Her smile is fucking stunning. Like I didn't know that already.

She sits there, on the chair next to me, one foot perched on the edge of the chair, her chin resting in her hand, and listens to me talk about my PhD and my thesis and all the boring engineering shit I do all day. But it doesn't seem to bore her, not at all.

She feeds me one of her crab rangoon, and the way she watches my mouth has me stirring again. This girl has drugged me. She slipped me a viagra, and I missed it. How else could I, a man of my age, be this turned on again, after coming five times already since midday?

"I guess we should go get my phone now," she says, licking her fingers clean and looking up at the clock, which shows it's already past ten. "And I should grab my clothes."

"Sure. I need to swing by the store, too."

"Why?"

I give her a grin. "Condoms. You're depleting my supply right quick."

She bites her lip and giggles. "Oh."

"Yes, oh."

"We could just go without?" She wiggles her shoulders playfully. "I *am* on birth control."

The thought is too tempting. Being able to just fuck her whenever, wherever for the weekend, it couldn't be that bad, could it? If she was on birth control, maybe it would - *No.*

"Yes, you are, but that's not infallible, and you are on the way to becoming a star bridge builder, and I won't risk you getting pregnant and interrupting that." I get to my feet and kiss her forehead. "Now come on, let's go get your phone."

———

The streets are quiet as I navigate my way through our neighbourhood and out to the highway. The next 24-hour store is a twenty minute drive away, and the roads are completely quiet. Amber sits beside me, a duffel bag of her clothes at her feet, and her phone in hand as she answers all the snaps and calls she missed while she was in my bed.

"Laurie was really freaking out," she says with a laugh. "She's such a worry wart."

"That she is."

"My parents got to Boston fine." She puts the phone down in the door of the car and turns to look at me. "I told them all I was asleep."

"Good." I reach over and take her hand, pressing it to my lips, which earns me a little giggle. "Can I ask you something?"

"Of course."

I inhale carefully and take the left-hand turn towards the highway. "You've said a few things, like about the 'I Love Yous', and anal sex, and just now with the choking." I cast a quick glance over at her, barely catching any of her features in the mostly dark car, before putting my eyes back on the road. "I don't mean to pry, but... Did this guy, I mean, did he hurt you?"

"If you're asking if he raped me, he didn't." She draws her knees up against her chest, and stares out the windshield with a sigh. "It wasn't like *that*. But... I don't know. I thought I was mature enough to know what I wanted and how to ask for it, but I was pretty inexperienced. I never had a boyfriend in high school. My mom was against me dating before I turned 18."

"And how do you feel about that?"

She sighs heavily and wraps her arms around her legs. "I understood it, or at least I tried to, but I also think she sheltered me too much. I went to college, and then I was surrounded by all these handsome men, not high school boys, and I was kind of star-struck, does that make sense?"

I nod and dart another quick glance in her direction to see her chewing her lip. "That makes complete sense, honey."

"I guess it didn't prepare me for what guys are like. I thought having three older brothers, I would know all about boys. But having boys in your family, and dating them, well... That's really not the same thing." She drops her head back against the headrest. "At all."

"No, I imagine it's not." I pause at the Stop sign, glancing over again, at this impossibly young woman whose voice is already weary with disappointment. "I'm sorry."

She rolls her head against the headrest to look at me, meeting my eyes for just a moment before I turn my attention back to the road.

"You don't have to be sorry."

"Yes, I do." I scratch my cheek with my thumb and sigh. "I hear shit like this too often, and it makes me wonder what part we men all play in it. Letting our buddies talk shit about women, all those off-colour jokes that you know are wrong, but you don't call them out, because it's *just a joke*, right?" I shrug, accelerating as the road meets the highway and the long stretch of black winds into the night ahead of us. "And then pretty girls like you go out into the world and feel like it's your fault for not being experienced, when really it's just asshole guys taking advantage of that."

Her hand is on my arm, stroking gently, and she lets out a soft laugh. "You really are the sweetest."

No I'm not. I'm an old man who's doing something he shouldn't, with a woman who's far too young for him.

But I'm not going to admit that to myself. I push those

thoughts down, far, far down and away, where they can't escape and shove reality into my stupid face. I take Amber's hand, and kiss it again, and again, as though holding that perfect, delicate hand to my mouth makes everything that happened to her alright, and everything I'm doing with her worth it.

I am a better man.

I won't hurt her.

I'll give her a fun time, a good weekend, and then I'll send her on her way knowing what she should expect from a man.

Nothing more.

The parking lot is practically empty as we pull up, hardly surprising considering the late hour, and a welcome relief knowing we definitely won't run into someone we might know. Amber huddles under my arm, letting me shield her against the icy breeze. She wraps her arms around my waist, and dammit, but it feels so good.

We amble through the aisles, completely relaxed, Amber cracking jokes and turning to kiss me every now and then. She grabs some snacks, an oversized bottle of cold brew coffee as well as some vanilla creamer. It feels so natural to keep my arm around her, to plant a kiss against her forehead, to ask her what flavor chips are her favourite.

Danger. Danger.

We get to the personal care section, and Amber giggles into my shoulder.

"Do they even sell extra extra extra large condoms here?" She asks, and leans up to nip my earlobe with her teeth.

I chuckle, and pick up the black and gold box marked King-Size.

"These fit me just fine." I toss them into the basket, and

Amber fixes me with a devious grin before plucking two more boxes from the shelf and tossing them in too.

"Just in case," she says, wrapping her arms around my neck and kissing me.

Right in the middle of the store, like this is a completely normal thing we can do. Her tongue strokes against mine, and I lock my free arm around her waist, lifting her up against me, and she hums appreciatively against my lips.

"We should get home," she murmurs, "unless you wanted to be my first fuck in a car?"

This girl is going to kill me.

"Fucking in a car is ridiculously uncomfortable," I say with a laugh, putting her back on her feet. "But maybe I just didn't find the right position?"

"Worth experimenting, don't you think?" She grins up at me, those warm brown eyes sparkling. She takes a hold of my hand, winding her long fingers through mine, and pulls me in the direction of the check-out. We place our items out on the belt, and Amber giggles as she stacks the three boxes of condoms. She backs into my chest, and takes my arm to wrap it around her waist. I drop a kiss to her temple as the cashier bags our things. The cashier looks at Amber, then at me, and raises an eyebrow.

"You all having a good night?" She asks, scanning the three boxes of condoms and tossing them into a blue plastic bag.

"If things work out," Amber says, stroking her fingers along my arm.

The cashier looks at me, and although she doesn't shake her head, her expression drips with judgment and displeasure. I avoid her eyes, fumbling in my back pocket for my wallet, pulling out my card and tapping it once the cashier gives me the total.

"You have a good night," I say to her, taking up the bags.

"God bless you." The cashier's voice is like taking a bullet to the gut.

Because God certainly wouldn't fucking bless whatever the hell this is.

Amber doesn't seem to notice anything, just maintains her happy, blissful demeanour, snuggling into me on the way back out to the car. She plants kisses on my neck, running her hand over my ass, and presses her mouth to mine when I open her door for her.

"So, about the fucking in the car?" She says with a grin before plopping down into her seat.

"You're incorrigible." I shake my head and laugh, closing the door and rounding the car to my side. I put the bags in the back seat, then get in and gun the engine.

Amber puts her hands to the heater, and shakes her shoulders. "It's gotten so cold already."

"Mmm, it has. I think it's going to be a long winter."

Once we're back on the highway, she turns to me in her seat. "Are you going to tell me more about this car fucking?"

"You sure you want to hear it?" I regard her with a raised eyebrow. "It's not a very exciting story."

"Yes I want to hear it! Tell me."

I chuckle and shake my head. "Well, once was in the backseat of my car in my last year of high school, and, well I mean I probably wasn't really great, and it was cramped, and she broke up with me the day after."

Amber laughs sympathetically, and puts a hand on my shoulder. "Oh no. I'm sorry."

"Ah, it's fine."

"And then?"

I hesitate to tell this part of the story, because... Well...

I take a deep breath, the night rolling past the car as we head back to my house. "Mella and I, we borrowed this camper from a friend in our second year of college and road-tripped down to South Carolina. It wasn't even really a camper, just an old car with a mattress in the back."

"I bet that was a lot more comfortable." Amber's voice isn't quite as jovial now. "Was that at least good?"

Yeah, it was. "I guess so, yeah."

Silence overtakes the car, and I wish to god I hadn't mentioned it. Why say it? Why bring up my damn ex-wife, the woman Amber knows just as well as she knows me, and mention us having sex? *Way to wreck the mood, Rembrook. Jesus.*

"Do you miss being married?" Amber asks after a while.

"No," I say quickly, shaking my head. "I mean, I miss parts of it. I miss having someone to come home to. Someone to sit with at night and talk about our day. Someone to sleep next to."

"Someone to fuck?"

I chuckle and nod. "Yes, that too. I miss that a lot. But I don't miss being married to *her*."

"Was she a bitch?"

"No, no I didn't mean it like that. Mella's a great person, we were both just... Not right for each other, I guess. We tried to make it work for a long time, especially for Laurie. But it just got to a point where we had to admit it wasn't going to happen. We were both miserable."

"Laurie said you two used to fight a lot."

I rub the back of my neck and wince. "I hate that she heard those arguments. They were so... So *stupid*. Nothing but two people picking at each other just to try and hurt the other one. It went on for way too long."

"I'm sorry." Amber puts a hand on my thigh, and it

doesn't even feel sexual, it just feels like comfort, like care. "But please, don't beat yourself up. Laurie loves both of you, and she tells me all the time what great parents you are."

I put my hand over Amber's, and give her a quick smile in the dark. "Thanks. I'm glad to hear it."

Amber keeps her hand on my thigh for the remainder of the drive home, and I love how it lets me know that she's there, just there for me.

Our neighborhood is silent when I pull into the drive of my house. As soon as I kill the engine, Amber unbuckles her seatbelt and throws herself over at me, taking my face in her hands and kissing me hungrily.

"Get in the back," she whispers.

"In the back?" I laugh, shaking my head. "I don't think-"

"Come on, get in the back." She pulls back from me and grins. "I have an idea."

I sigh heavily, and tell myself to stop being such a square. "Yes, ma'am." I heave myself over through the front seats, into the back, and I swear to god, if I get a cramp or put my back out or any other old man shit in front of this girl right now, I'm going to set my car on fire.

But by some stroke of luck, I make it without pulling any muscles, and throw myself down in the middle seat. Amber is in the front, peeling off her sweats, and she points to the bag beside me.

"Put on a condom," she says, shuffling off my oversized hoodie that she borrowed.

"I- Honey, I'm not- *Fuck*." Embarrassment scorches my cheeks because I'm not hard yet, and for one stupid, awful second, I worry that maybe I won't be able to perform. I free my flaccid dick from my jeans, and jerk myself, my lips bitten together with frustration.

Amber flops over the front seat with a grin. "You're not hard yet, baby?" She gets on her knees, and yanks up her white t-shirt. It's dark, the only light coming from the streetlight outside my house, but it's enough to see her perfect tits, nipples peaking in the cool air.

"Oh fuck," I grit out harshly, and yeah, I'm not broken, I should not have worried at all, because within two or three strokes I'm so hard my dick is practically glowing with heat.

Amber straddles the centre console of the car, one knee on either seat, and peels off the shirt completely. I worry for a second that she'll get cold, but with her completely naked *in my damn car*, my worries are quickly forgotten. I can't focus on anything else but her tits, and her legs, and her pussy that's right in front of me.

I tear at the packaging of the box of condoms, and Amber lets out a lascivious little laugh, like she can see that she's driving me crazy, and she loves it. She puts her middle and index fingers in her mouth, licking them, and then pushes them between the lips of her pussy.

Oh. Fucking. Hell.

I rip the condom packet open with my teeth, going completely against everything I was always taught about safe condom use, and roll the condom down over my dick. Where a second ago I was soft, I'm now so hard it's almost torturous. What is this girl doing to me?

Amber moans softly, still rubbing her clit in front of me.

"Oh," she whimpers. "*Oh*, Theo, I need you inside me."

"Come here," I order, and she smiles at me in the mostly dark car.

She climbs through the car seats, flipping herself around so her back is to my chest. She was soaked before, but that was with foreplay, with an orgasm or three. I didn't grab any lube, *shit why am I so stupid?* I spit on my fingers, and run them through her heat. I don't know why I was worried. My girl is so wet it makes the tip of my dick leak pre-cum.

I grip her hips, and she steadies herself with a hand on each of the front seats. I slide forward a little, not too far because there's not enough room for my legs, but I need to see, I want to watch as she lowers herself onto me. I fist the base of my cock, lining myself up with her entrance, and she whimpers, the muscles of her back contracting as she takes me in slowly.

Another moment of wondering just how the hell I ended up here, in the drive of my damn house, out here where anyone taking their dog for a midnight walk is going to see my car bouncing as Amber Pope fucks her best friend's dad in the backseat.

Amber takes a minute to lower herself all the way, and I stroke her back, her hips, as she does, telling her how beautiful she is, how good she feels. I don't think she'll be able to sink all the way down, to take all of me at this angle, but with a low, needy moan, she's in my lap, my cock filling her all the way. She's shaking lightly, and she rolls her head back and forth on her shoulders, testing her hips side to side, moaning and hissing in sharp breaths.

I can't even talk now. My head is back against the seat, my breath pounding out of me, and I watch as Amber lifts herself slightly, barely releasing an inch of me, before she lowers herself again. She repeats the motion a few times, and every time it feels like heading back through the gates of heaven. She's angelic, glowing and naked in the car, while I feel almost grotesquely large, sprawled out on this seat while she bounces on my cock.

"Fuck," I murmur, a strained sound in the car.

She turns her head, her lips parted as she pants. "Does that feel good?"

"Honey, it's... Fuck it's so far past good." I dig my hands into her hips, urging her to roll herself on me, needing more friction, more movement, just more, more of her, all of her. "You're so fucking tight."

"You're so big," she murmurs, bouncing harder. "You feel like, oh god, you feel like you could break me."

"Maybe I should break you." *What. The Fuck. Was that?* I don't know where this voice is coming from. I enjoy dirty talk, some light degradation, but this, what the fuck is this? I'm grabbing onto Amber's hips, helping her slam herself down onto me, and a growl echoes through my chest. "Maybe I should break this pussy so everyone knows it's mine, huh?"

You're a fucking animal, Rembrook.

But my girl is into it. She moans, a sound filled with need and pleasure and dizzying arousal. She throws her hair back, the cascade of copper trailing down in front of me, and I plunge a hand into her silky waves, tensing and flexing at the back of her head. My other hand moves to her breast, impossibly plump and round, her nipple a hard peak between my fingers.

My words unleashed something, because now I'm a possessive animal, my hips bucking to meet hers, spearing my cock into her cunt over and over.

"I used to... Oh I used to touch myself, thinking of you." She digs her hands into the seats, steadying herself as she picks up the pace.

"Oh yeah?" I wet my lips, gritting my teeth as the

amazing stabbing pressure in my groin gets stronger. "You played with your pussy thinking about me?"

"Yes. *Yes*." The pitch of her voice changes, and my hand skates down her stomach to where we're joined, where her skin is stretched around me, her clit swollen and needy. I'm probably too rough, too hard, but I pinch her clit between my fingers and she cries out.

"You're going to come for me, honey, and then I'm going to take you inside, and you're going to come for me again, and again, you understand?" I'm moving harder than she is now, slamming my hips up into her as she holds on, begging for *more, yes, there, oh god, Theo, Theo, don't stop, fuck me, fuck me*. I'm lost in her voice, in the motion of her body, in my own need that's racing down my spine in licking, white-hot flames.

"*Theo!*" She cries out, her hands falling from the seats and digging into my thighs, scrambling as her body releases, her orgasm storming through her, her body clamping around my cock. I see fucking stars for a second, and then I'm coming, Amber's body still quivering on top of me as her hips jerk, draining out my release.

She collapses back against me, and we're both breathing hard, both hot and spent. She turns her head to rest her forehead against my cheek as I wrap my arms around her waist.

"H-how.... Are you this good?" She asks breathlessly, swallowing hard and shaking her head. "Th-this is what I was missing out on, all this time?"

"That was all you, honey," I say with a laugh, stroking her hair that's sticking to the sweat on her forehead. "You were incredible."

She laughs, gasping a little as she moves her hips. "You're like a machine. You feel like... You feel like you're still hard." She reaches down, teasing the exposed length of my cock with her fingertips, and giggles when I suck in a breath. "Ready for more?"

"Absolutely, but not out here. You'll get cold."

She laughs again, a sweet, lyrical sound, and raises herself carefully off me. My cock falls back against my stomach, the condom filled, and I grimace at the thought of tucking myself away with it just to get back in the house. Amber yanks on the sweat pants and my hoodie, and we sneak back to the house like a pair of burglars. We scan the neighborhood for any sign of movement, any sign of someone who may have heard the screaming and moaning coming from my damn car.

But the windows around us are all dark, the houses quiet, only the cool wind rustling through the trees. Undiscovered once again.

Back in the house, I go to the downstairs bathroom to deal with the condom, which feels absolutely terrible now. I avoid my reflection, not wanting to be looking into the face of the man who just did that with Amber in his car.

I emerge into the kitchen to find her putting away the things we bought at the store, and she smiles over her shoulder at me.

"Just some housekeeping, then you can take me upstairs for more," she says with a grin.

Maybe you should stay forever so it can always be like this.

Another thought I quash quickly. Nope, we're not doing that. That's just the loneliness and the two years of not getting laid talking. Nothing else.

"Why don't we shower?" I say, and Amber nods.

"Sure. Shower sex sounds great."

———

Who needs the gym?

Weights? Why? When I have a voracious twenty-year-old naked in my shower? A beautiful woman who nips and bites at me the minute we're under the hot water? Who clamps her teeth down on my nipple, and holy fuck, I have a pain kink? Good to know.

Learning more and more about myself with every passing moment.

Amber's hands are all over me, tracing over my tattoos, her thumbs caressing my abs as she sighs. She's gorgeous like this, even more gorgeous, naked, slippery and skin turning pink in the warm steam.

Lifting her up against the shower wall, pressing myself against her while her hands cradle my face, and she kisses me, soft and slow - it's fucking bliss.

So good. Too good. Far too fucking good, because I forget myself for a second.

Our mouths still joined, tongues still sliding against each other, still tasting each other, I grasp the base of my cock and sink into her. She moans into my mouth, and an intoxicating combination of pleasure and panic seizes my brain.

Because I'm not wearing a condom.

I'm inside Amber, all the way, not just the tip like on my desk this afternoon - *was it only just this afternoon? Has it only been 12 hours?* - no, this time, I'm buried inside her, all the way, enveloped by her heat. I pull back from the kiss with a strained laugh, and she's gazing up at me, with that look, that look I hope no other man has ever seen before, her hooded eyes and plump, red lips.

"Sorry, honey," I murmur, trying to shift away from her. "I didn't think."

"It's OK." She locks her legs around my waist, keeping me there. "I told you, I don't mind."

"Amber-"

"Just for a minute." Her head tips back, her hair a mess of half-wet strands that stick to her cheeks and her shoulders. "Just stay inside me for a minute." She closes her eyes, moaning as she tenses the muscles inside her, and I grit my teeth hard, suppressing a groan.

"If you do that again, I'll come."

She giggles softly, looking like some devilish goddess, eyes still closed and mouth widened in a grin. "I'll be very good and stop that then." She opens her eyes just enough to look at me, to watch my face as I try to maintain my composure. "I feel that good?"

"Yes, you do." Heat prickles at my lips from the strain of holding back, of trying not to think too much about *how fucking good* it feels to be inside her raw.

"What if you just pulled out?" She asks, shifting her hips a little, which has me grasping her ass hard enough to leave handprints. "Before you come? Could you just do that?"

I don't fucking think I can.

I shake my head, and goddamn me, but I pull out a little, and thrust back inside her. Amber's eyes widen, and she gasps out an incoherent curse.

"I can't like this, honey, I..." The internal war within myself lasts approximately 14 milliseconds, but it feels like an eternity. I crush Amber's mouth with mine, not fucking her exactly, just pressing myself into her, and she writhes and squirms in my arms. I'm a good man. I know this is wrong. I know I should be responsible. I know I shouldn't gamble, not with her, not like this. *I'm a good man. I'm responsible...*

Fuck it.

I put Amber down on her feet, and her eyes flash up to mine with question before she lets out a delighted yelp as she's spun around and pressed against the tiles. I grip her hip with one hand, pressing the other to the small of her back, angling her peachy round ass towards me. She sucks in a ragged breath as I press the blunt head of my cock to her pussy.

As wrong as it is, as much as I know this is another mistake in a long line of mistakes I've made this afternoon, I push my naked cock inside her, on purpose, feeling every inch of heat and slickness pass my sensitive skin.

Amber lets out a long, low moan when my hips are sitting flush against her ass.

"Oh god, Theo." One of her hands is braced against the wall, the other massaging her nipple languidly.

"You like it like this, honey?" My thrust is probably too hard, too much for her, but all I'm met with is more moans. "You like me stretching this pussy of yours?"

"Yes," she murmurs, her head turned so I can see the flush rising in her cheeks, her eyes squeezed shut under the curtain of her wet hair.

"I want to fuck you hard, pretty girl." I pound into her again, and her mouth opens in an *O*, her back tensing. "Do you want me to do that?"

"Yes." It's a moan, a loud moan, a fucking plea of mercy. "Don't hold back, oh god, please."

I know I should hold back. I shouldn't be rough with her, not after what she just went through. I don't want to be another one in the list of men who treat her like shit, and hurt her. Yes, I want to fuck her, and chase that pressure, the choking feeling of her cunt around me, but I can't do that to her, can I?

"Please use me." The words drop from her mouth, and she mewls as she shifts her hips. The hand that was playing with her nipple moves down between her legs, and she begins to massage her clit. "Use me, Theo. I want to be used."

Fuck.

I'm a good man. I know I am. But right now, I'm not Theo Rembrook, jovial professor and father of one.

I'm a fucking animal.

It's rapturous, like entering another plane of existence, pounding that impossibly tight little pussy. Amber's not moaning anymore, her sounds are too loud for that, she's almost screaming. Each stroke, each clench of her body, each push back into her is a primal fight for ownership.

"This is what you wanted me for, isn't it, honey?" I'm not thrusting anymore, I'm *rutting*, the sharp angle of her hips not letting me slip too far out, her body greedily holding on to me. "To do what all those useless college boys couldn't do for you."

"Oh... *Oh.* Yes." She's snatching in breaths desperately, almost rasping, her brow pinched together and her full lips parted. "Theo. *Theo.*"

That begging, desperate tone is back, and I have no idea where the man I woke up as this morning has gone, but I don't care. I lose the ability to speak, because Amber raises herself on her tiptoes, screaming and crying out, the sound reverberating up the tiled walls, and with a strangled *Fuck*, she comes, and I want to say things to her I haven't said in years. That I maybe haven't said ever, because my brain is misfiring as my balls draw up tight and my own orgasm begins to stab through me.

You're mine. This pussy belongs to me. I'm going to fucking ruin you for any other man. You'll be begging for my cock. You'll be crying because no one can fuck you as good as I can.

The carnality of my thoughts doesn't cease when I pull out of her throbbing pussy with a groan, and I angrily stroke my cock over her ass. I press my other hand against the wall over her head, the tip of my dick hitting Amber's skin over and over, then with a harsh grunt, I explode. One jet after another coats her ass, hot, sticky and all-consuming. It's frustrating, a completely disappointing orgasm after being choked and clenched inside her.

In the light of day I could still rationalise, I could still be the responsible lover who used protection and respected this arrangement. But now, in the deep of the night, all of that has disappeared. As my mind starts to clear, I look down at Amber's shivering frame, her hands flat against the wall. I'm still panting, trying to catch my breath, and really look at what I've done to her.

It's filthy. It's primal. It's beautiful.

And I fucking hate myself for it.

Wordlessly, I lather up a loofah and start to clean my cum off Amber's ass. She makes a small sound, somewhere between a moan and a sigh, and straightens up. She presses her front to the wall and wiggles her hips slightly.

"Oh god," she breathes.

I don't know what to say. I should be saying something. I should be talking her through it. I should be telling her how good she did. I should be fucking on my knees thanking her for letting me do that to her, for using her for my own pleasure like a goddamn sex doll.

I'm sure she's going to turn around and slap me, tell me to go fuck myself, and never look at me again.

Then a low, throaty laugh breaks from her as she stretches her arms up the wall.

"Can we do that again?"

When I don't respond, she turns around, that sex-drunk, happy look draining from her face.

"Theo?"

I can't meet her eyes. I can't admit to all the thoughts I just had, all the things I wanted to do, that I wanted from her, while I was buried inside her. So I keep washing her, shame and guilt plunging into the pit of my stomach.

"Theo?" She takes my face in her hands, trying to meet my gaze. "What's wrong?"

When I finally relent and look at her, I see nothing but concern. With a sigh, I wrap my hands around her wrists gently, stroking the backs of her hands with my thumbs.

"I didn't want to hurt you."

She shakes her head. "But you didn't."

"Really?"

Her face lights up with a smile as she eagerly nods. "Really. It felt amazing. *You* felt amazing. I loved every minute of it."

"I... I felt like I was using you."

Amber laughs softly. "I did kind of tell you to. It's my fantasy, remember?"

"Yes, but-"

"Stop." She raises her lips to mine, kissing me gently, with complete trust. "Stop freaking out. You're not going to corrupt me with your dick, I promise." She smiles when I huff out a laugh. "It felt really good. And I meant it, I wish we could do it again."

I stroke her cheek with the backs of my fingers. "Me, too."

"Then we know what we're doing with our day tomorrow, right?" She wraps her arms around my neck and kisses me, long, slow, soft, warm.

And I still don't tell her what I was thinking. That she's somehow unleashed some feral, possessive side of myself that I didn't even know was there anymore. That I want to fuck her until Monday - and then for all the days after that.

Which, of course, I can't.

On Monday, I will have to let her go, and I'll have to tell myself that I haven't possibly fallen for this girl in the space of less than a day. We agreed it was just sex. Nothing is going to change. We sure as hell aren't going to fall in love.

3

SATURDAY MORNING

Rain wakes me first, the steady pattering against the window drawing me from my dreams.

And straight into another one.

Amber is lying beside me, stretched out and heavenly, her hair in a wild array on the pillow. The comforter has slipped down to reveal her breasts, and I could wake up to this sight every day and never get tired of it.

My self-loathing from last night eased a little with Amber's reassurance, but I still can't get those possessive thoughts out of my head. I have no right to entertain them, I know that. I know better than to have one amazing night with a pretty girl send me into a tailspin.

I have to banish that sentimental, foolish side of myself for the remainder of the weekend, to be dealt with on Monday when this is all over. For now, I want to be what Amber wants, the man she needs me to be, the one to give her the experience she deserves.

Amber murmurs in her sleep and rolls over onto her stomach. Because I'm a greedy bastard, I want to see more, and I pull the comforter down so I can take in more of her. I lean over to inhale the warm scent of her skin, downright greedy for it, and as my palm caresses the curve of her ass, I trail kisses down her spine. She smells like heaven, like cotton and sandalwood soap, and a bit of me, the scent of my cologne clinging to her hair.

She stirs, sighing sleepily into her pillow, brushing aside the hair that trails over her face. She shifts her hips, pressing her ass against my palm, and makes a hum of satisfaction.

"I like waking up like this," she says, stretching her arms out, and reaching back to stroke a hand along my stomach. "I read a book a couple months ago, and it was all about somnophilia." She raises her head a little, giving me a sideways smirk. "You know what that is?"

"I do, as a matter of fact." My kisses trail lower, to the small of her back, my hands now kneading the firm flesh of her ass. "Is that another thing you'd like to try?"

"Not like, with sedation or anything," she says with a small laugh, and another hum rings through her as my hands stray lower, over her upper thighs and down into the valley between her legs. "Just like... waking up with a cock inside me. I think that'd be fun."

I file this information away for later, because that does sound like fun, and the thought of a sleeping Amber lying in my bed, peaceful and vulnerable, turns me on more than it should. My reason tells me I should show some restraint and not spend the entire weekend just fucking this girl, but then... Isn't that what she wanted? Isn't that exactly what she's here for?

"Have you ever filmed yourself?" Amber asks, raising herself on her elbows and tossing her long copper hair over her shoulder.

I laugh against her skin, my thumbs teasing along the

seam of her cunt, and she tenses, biting her lip with a sharp intake of breath.

"I remember a polaroid camera being involved one time, but no, no filming." I gaze up at her, along the slope of her back, and raise an eyebrow. "Somnophilia, free use, now voyeurism? Pretty girl has quite a list of kinks growing there."

Amber giggles, pressing the backs of her fingers against her mouth. "Are you horrified yet?"

"Honey, nothing about you could horrify me."

"Oh, don't say that." Amber folds her arms on the pillow and lays her head down on them. "I don't need to be on a pedestal."

"Unless that pedestal is my face."

She lets out a throaty, lecherous laugh. "Now *that's* a pedestal you can put me on, any time. Though I might smother you."

"If it's your pussy that kills me, I will die a happy man." My fingers probe a little further between her legs, and she's so warm here, a warmth that makes me want to bury my face and lick her to orgasm before we even have breakfast.

"I can see the headstone now," she says with a sigh, parting her legs a little more for me. "Here lies Theo Rembrook, who died doing what he loved."

"Mmm, that's right." I lick my fingers, raising myself and feeling too damn smug at the expression on her face as I push my wet fingers inside her. "Now, tell me more about wanting to be filmed."

Amber squirms and a tiny moan passes her lips. "I... I thought it'd be kind of hot..."

I press my fingers deeper, and she whimpers.

"Yes, Amber? What did you think would be hot?"

"To... be filmed, from behind... So..." She trails off as I

withdraw my fingers to massage her clit. "No one would know it's me, or you. But just... like a little souvenir. So we'd know it was us. And we could always remember what we'd done, and how good it felt."

My heart does a fucking somersault. She hasn't just dreamed of being filmed, she's dreamed of being filmed with *me*. Goddamn I am a fool. A fucking old fool.

"You thought about this a lot?" I stretch away from her for a minute, and she raises her head to see what I'm doing, a smile tugging her at her lips as I retrieve a bottle of lube from the night stand. I move behind her, kneeling between her thighs, which she's now spread wide open for me. "You thought about being able to watch our own video, over and over?"

She tries to turn over, but I hold her steady with a flat hand to her back.

"You stay like this, honey," I say softly, and she settles back down. I take my hard cock in my hand, and spread lube over the tip. "I want you just like this."

Now that I'm all slick, I brace one hand beside her, and guide my hips between her thighs. Last night I was panicked, so worried about being inside her without protection, but today? Today I don't care, and she doesn't care. Those three boxes of condoms are going to go to waste.

I can live with that.

"What do you like to masturbate with?" I ask as I nudge at her entrance, and it's a tight fit at this angle. Even with the lube, I have to squeeze and press my shaft inside her, the pressure around the tip of my cock enough to have me closing my eyes and taking a deep, steadying breath. "What toys do you have?"

"I... I have a dildo," she says, her fingers grasping onto the edges of the pillow. "It's... it's not as big as you."

"No one can fill this greedy cunt like I can, isn't that right, honey?"

That felt like too much. The possessive asshole is coming back, and I try to push him away as I ease in, further and further.

Amber shakes her head against the pillow. "I've... never been as full as I have with you."

"What else?" I lean down to plant a kiss on that spot, that soft patch of skin behind her ear, and chuckle as she shivers. "What else do you do when you need this pussy looked after?"

"I... I have a, uh, a little sucker, for my clit." She moans as I bottom out inside her. "Oh fuck, Theo, that's-"

"You lie on your back when you use it?" The image of Amber splayed out on a bed, with a toy between her legs and a hand on one of her perfect tits, swims before my eyes. It's such a fucking delicious thought that I know I could come right here and now if I surrender to it.

But I'm not wearing a condom, and we're playing the pull-out game.

Restraint, asshole. Practice some damned restraint.

Amber shakes her head again, lifting her head a little, panting lightly. "No, I... I like to, oh, I straddle it. I kneel on my bed, and... I use it like that."

"Just like you were sitting on my face, huh?" I rock in and out of her slowly, taking my time, because this time I'm not a feral animal using her body in the shower. This time I'm enjoying every stroke, the gentle release then the blissful, agonising slide back inside her. "You want to fuck my mouth?"

"Yes." She nods, and as she lifts her chest from the bed, I

reach under her to roll her breast in my hand. "I want... I want to know what that feels like."

"It feels so good, honey." Her breath catches in her throat as I increase my pace, long, hard strokes that have her whimpering and mewling with need. "You'd be rolling this needy little cunt on my face, fucking my tongue, because nothing has ever felt as good."

"Not even as good... as this?" She laughs breathlessly, her hands flexing on the pillow, and she winces as I slam into her. "Because, this feels... This feels so good."

"So needy for my cock, aren't you, pretty girl?" I suppress a gasp myself, because my head is starting to swim and my release is close, too close because she's holding me so tight inside her. "Walking into my house with no panties on, acting so innocent when you were wet and greedy for me."

She moans, squeezing her eyes closed, shifting her hips to meet each one of my thrusts. The pillow is clenched into her closed fists, her thighs squeezing together as her whole body tenses, the storm of her release threatening to tip her over the edge. And *fuck*, if that doesn't just have me fucking losing it.

I want to stay inside her, because she's close, so fucking close, but it's too tight, too hot, too good, and *I can't, I can't, I can't*. With a frustrated grunt I pull out, and I'm met with an agonising moan as Amber shakes beneath me. I rise to my knees, stroking my cock and barely needing to, because already the pressure is so much, so hard, heat and tension tearing at the base of my spine.

Then Amber lifts her hips, her manicured fingers rolling over her clit. If I wasn't already on the brink, I sure would be now.

My release spills out of me, lashing Amber's raised ass

with one rope after another of hot cum. I watch as it runs down between the cleft of her ass, over her swollen, pink skin, and down, down to meet her fingers. Amber is masturbating herself to orgasm with my cum as lube and it's the hottest thing I've ever seen in my life.

I stay where I am, hand wrapped around my still-hard cock, and watch, mesmerised, as Amber cants her hips more and more, giving me the perfect view as she starts to spasm. Her pussy pulses hard, and she moans *Theo, Theo* as her orgasm crests.

And god help me, I'm a fucking weak man.

Because just as she lets out a long, sharp cry into the bed, I slam my cock back into her.

———

We don't talk about it at all. Amber doesn't mention it. And the niggling voice that tells me spurting my... My lover's bare pussy with cum probably wasn't a good idea - that voice gets locked away along with my judgmental inner asshole, and the thoughts of Amber's father murdering me for dicking down his daughter.

For now, Amber's curled up in an armchair, wearing nothing but an oversized cardigan, a cup of coffee wrapped in her hands, smiling at me as I sit down in the armchair beside hers.

"I love this view," she says, gazing out the window before us. "I know it's just trees, but it's so pretty."

"It's what sold me on this house." I run a hand over my bare chest, the warmth of the fire washing over us both. "This view. It brought me a lot of peace."

"I bet." Amber takes a sip of her coffee, and tilts her

head as she looks back at me. "Do you think you'll ever get married again?"

"Me?" I chuckle, shaking my head. "Oh honey, I think I'm too old for all that."

She rolls her eyes and gags. "You *need* to stop with the 'I'm old, soooo old' line. You're in your 40s. You could live another 60 years."

"You got a whole lot of faith in my genes there," I say with a laugh, gulping down a warming mouthful of milky coffee.

"My grandpa is in his 90s, and still jogs, every day." Amber raises her eyebrows as though making an extremely valid point. "And you're a machine. Look how fit you are." Her expression shifts and she drags her lower lip through her teeth. "If you were so old, you could have never fucked me, what, 7 times in the past 18 hours?"

A flush rises in my face, and I rub the back of my neck as I laugh. "Yeah alright, you have a point. I don't do too bad for a man my age, I guess."

"You do extremely well." Amber smirks at me over the edge of her cup. "Besides, a hot guy like you? It's a waste for you to be single."

"I guess we'll see then." I shrug, looking over her long legs that are drawn up against her chest. "And what about you?"

Her eyebrows shoot up. "Me?"

"Yeah, you know, obviously you have the career all set for you, Miss Amber Pope, Master Bridge Builder, but what about the rest?" I wave my hand vaguely around the room. "You know, home and marriage and kids, is that all on the horizon for you?"

Amber sighs as she looks out the window at the slate-grey sky and the falling rain. "Marriage, yeah, maybe. If I met the right guy. But kids, no." She shakes her head adamantly. "I mean, don't get me wrong, I love them. My eldest brother and his wife have two year old twins, and they are *adorable*. I love them so much, but I don't really have the urge to be a mom myself. I'd rather be the rich, cool auntie that takes them to Disney, y'know?" She gives me a devious side glance. "Drops them off back home hyped up on sugar, that kind of thing."

I chuckle quietly and nod. "Fair enough."

"You and Mella never wanted any more? Kids I mean?"

I shift back into the armchair with a heavy breath, and squint at the sky. "No, no, we were happy with Laurie."

"I don't think anyone has more kids because they're unhappy with the first one." Amber leans towards me, reaching out a hand to stroke along my arm. "Laurie said once that she was an accident?"

"Oh, god no." I rub my forehead and shake my head. "No, she was, no I hate that word, *accident*. She was unplanned, but when we found out she was on her way, we were happy." I sigh, putting my coffee cup down on the side table, and suddenly I want to tell this young woman at my side everything. Things I've never really talked to anyone else about. "Mella had an abortion, real early on when we were first together. We were both still in college, and it was just the wrong time."

"Was that... hard for you?" Amber strokes her hand down my arm until she reaches my fingers, and entwines her own through them.

"No, no it wasn't. Mella was very matter-of-fact about it, and I sure as shit wasn't ready to be a father then, I was way too young." I smile over at her. "Just a little older than you are now."

Amber shakes her head with a huffed laugh, but doesn't

let go of my hand. "But then when she was pregnant with Laurie, it was the right time?"

I shrug, looking down at our joined hands and thinking how nice it is just to hold someone's hand. I wrap Amber's hand in both of mine, running my thumb over her delicate, long fingers, her pale peach manicured nails, and without thinking, raise her hand to my mouth to place a kiss in her palm.

Amber's expression when I meet her eyes is one of quiet surprise. She stares at me for a moment, then drops her gaze and turns away from me.

"Sorry," I mumble quickly, and her head whips back around to look at me.

"For what?"

"For... Um..." I don't even know why I'm apologising, but something just shifted in the room, and I'm sure it's my fault. "I feel like I just made you uncomfortable."

"By kissing my hand?" Amber scoffs, putting her cup down on the side table and drawing her legs up tighter against her chest, and wrapping her arms around them. "Why would that make me uncomfortable?"

"Amber, what just happened?"

"Nothing," she snaps, and dashes her hand across her face. It takes me a beat to realise that she's starting to cry.

"Honey." I kneel down in front of her, but she won't look at me. "What's going on?"

"I... I don't know." She shakes her head, chewing on her lip and angrily rubbing her face against her shoulder to stem the flow of more tears down her face. "I'm being stupid."

"No you're not. Something got to you, what is it?"

"You're just... You're so nice." Her head drops against her knees, and her shoulders shake as she starts to cry.

I reach out to take her hands, and suddenly she's on the ground, wrapped around me and sobbing into the crook of my neck. I hold her, stroking her hair, whispering comforting words to her as she cries her heart out.

I don't know how long we sit like that, but finally she calms and quiets, all her tears cried out.

"I'm so sorry," she murmurs, turning her head against my shoulder to gaze up at me. "You probably think I'm crazy, huh?"

"Crying doesn't make you crazy, honey. If you'd run around my house screaming bible verses, I'd probably be a little worried, but crying, I can handle."

Amber's face breaks into a smile, and she covers her ruddy face with her hand as she laughs. "I've never even read the bible."

I puff out an exaggerated sigh of relief. "*Good*. Because the last woman I let in here who had, she was *terrifying*."

Amber keeps laughing against my chest, then sits up and rubs her face with the sleeve of her cardigan. "God, I'm so embarrassed."

"Please don't be," I say, stroking her cheek with my thumb. "I just need to know you're OK. And if I did anything to bring that on."

She shakes her head and sniffles. "You didn't. I promise you didn't. It was just..." She exhales shakily, and wets her lips with her tongue. "The last time... The last time I slept with James, my um, I guess my ex-boyfriend, it was... I told you he didn't rape me, but that last time, I guess it felt like I was out of control, but in a bad way?"

Great. Last night did fuck her up. Nice one, Rembrook.

"Amber, I am so sorry if I did anything last night that-"

She takes my face in her hands and shakes her head. "No no no, Theo, listen to me, that's not what I meant." She places a hasty kiss on my lips, and she tastes like saltwater from her tears. "With James, it was never about me. I know that now. And the morning after... I was telling him that I wasn't comfortable, and that what had happened had... hurt." Her brow furrows, and rage swells in my chest. "I told him that he'd hurt me, he'd pushed me too far, and I needed him to not do that again. And he told me..." She inhales through her nose. "He told me that if I wanted to ever have a man who would stick around, I'd have to get used to it. Because all men wanted that."

I'm so angry I can't talk for a minute. My tongue is heavy and laced with venom in my mouth. I want to find this little punk James and beat the ever living shit out of him. I want to kill some college kid and bury him in a pit so deep he's never found.

Easy, there. Calm down. Focus on Amber.

"You know he's full of shit, right?" I lace my fingers into Amber's hair and look into her eyes. "You don't owe a man anything, especially nothing sexual, in order to keep him. Anyone who expects that isn't worth keeping."

"I know." She nods, then laughs breathlessly. "I mean, I do now. You, doing that last night, it felt like I was doing that *with* you. You know what I mean?"

I nod slowly. "You said you wanted to do all these things with someone you trust, someone who wouldn't hurt you, and then you discovered that you can do those things-"

"And have coffee made for me in the morning." Amber smiles softly, and brushes her fingers over my forehead. "Have my hand kissed. Have a sexy, smart, muscly man tell me his innermost thoughts." Her warm brown eyes search my face, and she smiles as she shakes her head. "I knew you'd be good to me. And I was so nervous yesterday, coming over here. Thinking you'd still see some kid that used to drink all your orange juice and put on bad music."

"You're not that kid anymore, honey." I run a finger under her cardigan, slipping it from her shoulder, and brush my lips over her warm, bare skin. "You're a woman. A beautiful, smart, funny, witty, ridiculously sexy woman, who has the whole world at her feet. Me included."

She laughs softly, letting me kiss her, letting me peel the cardigan off her body, letting me hold her, naked, warm and inviting, in my lap. I lay her out in front of the fire, and spend an eternity kissing her all over, not wanting to miss an inch of her. She lies there, her arms stretched out over her head, eyes closed, and it feels like renewal. Like she's cleansed herself of something, the bad that was weighing her down, and now that's all been released, she can be more herself.

Or maybe I'm just attributing too much to the power of my dick and I'm horny as fuck again.

But I take it slow. After what she confided in me, I don't want to rush her back into sex. She'll let me know when she's ready for that. For now, I just savour the taste of her skin, the small sounds she makes as my mouth continues to roam over her.

And then the fucking doorbell rings.

Amber's eyes fly open, wide as they meet mine.

"Who the fuck is that?" She hisses, and I grunt out my frustration before dropping a quick kiss to her lips.

"Stay right here."

I get to my feet, heading out into the hallway, yanking a sweater from the banister and pulling it on over my head. It's thankfully long enough to hide my raging erection, and I take a deep breath to stop myself punching whoever is ringing my damn doorbell square in the face. I tear the door open, and there stands Kathy Coleman.

Who lives right next door to Amber's parents.

"Morning Kathy," I say with a wide smile, trying my best to relax, *just fucking relax and act natural.* "Here for a cup of sugar?" *Jackass.*

"I'm sorry to bother you, Theo, but I'm a little worried." Kathy wrings her hands and glances past me into the house. "Is Laurie home?"

"No, she's in Connecticut with her mom, seeing her grandparents, why?"

"Now, you'll probably think I'm being silly, but last night, I was out with the dog, it was very late, and I swear I saw Amber go to her house." She glances around us furtively, and leans closer. "With a *man.*"

Fucking holy shitting hell.

"Oh." It's all I can say, and I frown, trying to think as my heart does laps around my entire nervous system and my brain melts into a puddle somewhere near my asshole. "I, uh, I don't know. I can ask Laurie to call her, if you're worried. Did you, uh, did you try the door? Is she home?"

Kathy nods. "Yes, I did, of course, but there was no answer, and her parents are down in Boston. I don't want to call and worry them if it's nothing."

"No, definitely, you don't want to call them, no, not over something like this." *No, that would probably be bad, very bad.* "I wouldn't worry, Kathy. I'll tell Laurie to check in on her, and everything'll be fine." I give Kathy a nod. "Right?"

Kathy shifts on her feet, and shakes her head. "It's just so strange, you know, Amber's a good girl, and her mother would never approve of her having a man in the house, I mean, it's just so unlike her!"

"Maybe it was just a friend from college." My grin feels

maniacal. I'm sure it looks it. "It was probably completely innocent."

"Morning Mrs Coleman!"

The bright voice from the driveway nearly gives me a heart attack. Kathy and I both look over at the same time, to see Amber in sweats, one earbud still in her ear, the other in her hand, her hair piled on her head. She waves to us both, a big smile on her face.

"Morning, Mr Rembrook!" Amber's eyes meet mine, bright and sparkling.

"Amber!" Kathy throws her hands up. "What are you doing jogging in this weather?"

"I just needed to stretch my legs, Mrs Coleman. I had a long drive yesterday." She raises a hand and waves, jogging past the house, then stops short. "Oh, Mr Rembrook?"

Speak. Speak. I clear my throat and fix a smile on my face. "Y-yes, Amber?"

"I think Laurie still has my Converse in her room, can I come in and check?"

My eyes flash to Kathy's face, but her expression is neutral. Of course, why would it be weird for my *daughter's best friend* to ask to come into my house? My guilt is beating me over the head, and I nod, sweeping a hand past me.

"Sure, come on in."

"Thanks!" Amber jogs to the door, then stops to jab a thumb over her shoulder. "Oh, Mrs Coleman? I think Ollie got out of your yard, I saw something white and furry running towards the park."

Kathy's eyes widen. "That damn dog!" She breaks into a run, across my drive and out into the street, in the direction of the park.

Amber turns back to me, smiling sweetly, her hands

clasped behind her back, just like they were when she appeared at my door yesterday afternoon.

"So, can I come in, *sir*?" She purrs, batting her eyelashes.

"Sure." I step aside, and she slips in past me. I slam the door, and Amber yelps as I grab her arm and yank her back against me. "How did you sneak out of the house so fast?"

Amber giggles softly, relaxing into me. "I'm just very, very clever."

"Yes, you are." I kiss her neck, shoving a hand under her sweater and finding her braless. "Did Mrs Coleman's dog really get out?"

"Oh, no. I must have been mistaken." She reaches back over her shoulders, clasping her hands around the back of my neck. "I could have sworn it was her dog."

"You're devious." I run both hands up under her shirt, over her soft smooth skin, and she exhales shakily as I massage her breasts. "So, so devious, pretty girl. I might have to punish you."

"Do I need a spanking, *sir*?"

Dammit, the way she says that, it has me hard in an instant.

"Do you think you need a spanking, Amber?" I pinch her nipples, hard, and she lets out a squeak. "Do I need to put you over my knee?"

"I-I made poor Mrs Coleman run all that way," she murmurs, her hips rolling against me, and she laughs with lecherous glee as she finds me already stiff and hard for her. "I probably need to be put in my place."

"You definitely do." I should be mortified that we nearly got caught. The guilt and shame that should be a clear sign to just stop what we're doing, is instead morphing into something else. Something thrilling and forbidden, that just makes this all more fun. Like bungee jumping. Like skydiving. It's all just a rush, some devious, depraved sport, and almost 24 hours into this weekend of experience, I want nothing more than to just keep playing. "Now, Miss Pope, I'd like to take you to my office and play a little game with you."

Amber sucks in a short breath. "A game, sir?"

"Yes, Miss Pope, a game." I walk her into my office, stopping in the middle of the room, facing my desk. I put my hands under her sweater and peel it off over her head. "Now, this is going to be a fun little fantasy, just for you and me, do you understand?" I sink to my knees, and roll her sweatpants down her legs.

"I understand, sir."

She's falling into this little fantasy way too easily, and I wonder just how many times she's had this exact scenario already play out in her head. *Bad, bad Theo.* Shut the fuck up.

Amber steps out of the sweats, and stands demurely with her hands folded in front of her, dressed in nothing but her white lacy panties. Her eyes are glowing with lust as I take off my own sweater, throwing it to the ground before putting on my glasses and taking a seat behind my desk.

"I want you to pick a safe word, Miss Pope."

She bites her lip, eyes scanning the floor before they pop back up to mine. "Bridge."

"Bridge. Understood." I rub my hand along my thigh. "Now, have you ever been punished like this before?"

She shakes her head.

"But you think you might like it?"

She nods. "Yes, sir."

"Good."

She hooks her thumbs into her panties, and I tut, wagging my finger as I frown.

"Did I say to take those off?"

She stops instantly, and drops her hands back to her sides. "No, sir. Sorry, sir."

"Good girl." I curl two fingers and beckon her to me. "Now, come here."

She takes a step, and I tut again, stopping her in her tracks.

"Not like that, Miss Pope. You're being punished."

She's too good at this, she understands the game too fucking well, and goddamn it makes me so hard there's no blood left anywhere in my body, it's all drained to my engorged cock. Because Amber drops to her hands and knees, keeping her eyes on me as she crawls across the floor towards me.

"Is this better, sir?" She purrs.

"Much better."

She crawls slowly, deliberately, and it makes me question which one of us is in control. Amber is so measured, so cool and collected even in the face of something she's never done before, and I'm almost bursting out of my skin in anticipation.

Sweet little innocent Amber knows exactly what she's doing.

She crawls to my side, and sits back on her folded legs, hands in her lap, gazing up at me with wide eyes.

"Now," I say, spreading my legs. "You'll lie across my lap. And you'll count them out with me."

"Count them?"

"Yes, Miss Pope. How many do you think you deserve?"

She chews on her lip. "Five?"

"I think that sounds right. Now." I gesture to my lap,

and she drapes herself across me, laying her mostly naked body over my legs, curling her arms under her. "Remember your safe word, honey."

She nods, and I can see that she's quivering. I am too, because it's been a long time since I did this with anyone. I forgot how much I like to dominate. How much I like to be in control. Or at least, how much I think I am in control, because Amber sure as fuck directed this.

My sweet, kinky girl.

I loop my thumb into the panties and yank them down, baring her ass. Amber puffs out a little gasp, her whole body on edge as she waits for the strike of my hand, for the pain or pleasure or both. I rub my hand over her ass, and growl low in my throat.

"Such a pretty ass you have, Miss Pope."

"Thank you, sir."

"I'm going to spank you now, understood?"

She nods quickly. "Yes, sir."

Smack

All the muscles in her back contract, her legs tensing. She holds her breath for a second, her trembling fingers digging into my thigh. I wait for her to count, to let me know she's still in the scene and not overwhelmed.

"One," Amber chokes out.

"One." I rub my hand over the place where my hand landed, which is going pink.

She's still tense, and her breathing is coming in short, sharp gasps. But she doesn't recoil at my touch. She's not shaking anymore. And when she lets out a little sigh, I strike again.

Smack

"Two!" Her voice is higher pitched this time, and she lets out a shaky moan.

"Two." I watch as she rubs her thighs together, her hips rolling to lift her ass higher.

Smack

"Three."

"Three." I run a hand over her head. "Remember your safe word, Miss Pope."

"I-I don't need it."

Fuck, but she's beautiful. Laid out over me like this, completely trusting me, trusting me not to hurt her, not to push her too far. I run my hand down the curve of her back, and maybe, just maybe I'm discovering things about myself again too, remembering who I am and what I like.

Not just someone's dad.

Someone's boss.

Someone's teacher.

No. In this moment, I feel more myself than I have in years. Yeah, yeah, it's not just because this beautiful, naked woman is lying in my lap. It's more than that. It's remembering there's more to me than just *that*, the public face, the family man, the responsible engineer.

As much as Amber trusts me, I trust her, too. To see this side of me. The freedom is intoxicating.

The fourth strike has her unravelling, and her hands scramble against my thigh. With a panicked gasp, she lifts her hips and tries to shove a hand between her legs. I seize her wrist, and she whines softly.

"We're counting, Miss Pope."

"F-four," she whimpers, rolling her chest to rub her breasts on my leg. "Fuck, Theo-"

"What's your safe word, Miss Pope?" I'm not going to break this scene unless she tells me it's too much. I don't want to ruin it for her and I'm not going to patronize her by assuming she can't take it. I keep a hold of her wrist until she stops shaking, and she takes a deep breath. "Miss Pope?"

"Four." Her voice is strained, and she's quivering lightly, but she settles back down on my lap. "That was four, sir."

"Yes it was." I caress her ass with my palm. "We're almost through with your punishment. You're doing so well, Miss Pope."

She hums out a high-pitched *Mmm*, and when my hand lands again, her back arches, her hips rolling desperately, and she whimpers.

"Five," she cries, panting.

"Five." I rub her ass, soothing the patch of skin that's now blooming red. "I'm so proud of you."

She takes a deep breath, and nods. "Thank you, sir."

"What are you feeling now?"

"I-I..." She trails off, and I let her gather herself, find her bearings. "I'd like to be fucked, please."

I run a hand over her ass, between her legs, and she mewls as my fingers find her centre.

"You're very, very wet, Miss Pope," I say, pushing two fingers into her hot pussy. "Did being punished like that turn you on?"

She nods frantically. "Yes, sir."

"Did almost being caught by your neighbour turn you on?"

She wasn't expecting that. Her shoulders draw up, and her breathing quickens. "Y-yes."

I chuckle quietly, swirling my fingers inside her. "Did it make you wet walking to my house with no panties on, past all those people, knowing you wanted to come here to fuck me?"

She's breathing hard now, her upper body taut and her

legs pressing together around my hand, trying to catch my fingers and ride me.

"No one has any idea just what a bad girl you are, do they, Miss Pope?"

She doesn't answer, just rocks her hips on my hand.

"Imagine if they saw you now, fucking my hand like this, like a greedy little slut."

Shit. Too far, too fucking far, Rembrook, what are you doing?

Amber whimpers, a sound that almost sounds like a sob. I take a deep, silent breath so as not to let on that I'm clambering on to my own restraint. *Check in on her, make sure she's doing good.*

"Do you like being called a greedy little slut, Miss Pope?"

She shakes her head, and immediately an apology bubbles up in my throat, but she's gasping, lifting her head, and with trembling lips she says, "I'm *your* little slut."

Well, holy fucking shit. I grit my teeth, arousal taking over my body, as well as my heart and my lungs that are now threatening to explode straight out of me. *Maintain. Stay in the moment, Give the girl what she asked for.*

"That's right," I murmur, stroking her hair. "You're *my* greedy little slut."

She lays her cheek on my thigh, nodding her head up and down, and her brows pinch together as my fingers continue to work her pussy. She's so wet now, soaking my hand, and riding my fingers hard. I'd love to continue this game, deny her the orgasm she needs, make her wait and be on the edge and needy and desperate for the rest of the day.

But that's too much for right now. Those are games for another day.

My heart sinks for a split second, because there won't be any more days after this weekend.

But I shake that off as Amber whimpers desperately, rocking her hips back and forth with more and more urgency.

"That's my girl," I croon, stroking her back. "Take what you need. Make yourself come. You deserve it after how well you did."

She might like degradation, but the praise has her moaning. She crosses her legs to catch my hand tightly, my fingers pressing and rubbing her g-spot. She shudders, tossing her head, and lets out a frustrated grunt.

"M-more," she grits out. "I need more."

"What do you need?" I keep my voice even, although my chest is pounding with the exertion of maintaining control. "I want you to use your words, and tell me what it is you need."

She chokes out another sob-like moan, pushing her hips back on my fingers.

"I-I..." She draws in a hard breath, more frustrated growls and groans. "I need to come."

"Do you want my mouth, or my cock?"

She inhales sharply, considering for a second. "I-I want your cock. Please."

"I know you do, honey. No one can make you come like I can, can they?"

"No," she breathes. "Please Theo, I need to come, please."

I withdraw my fingers from her cunt, and lick her off them, her taste coating my tongue. I stroke a hand over her hair again, and she sighs.

"Bend over the desk. Legs spread for me."

She scrambles from my lap, bending over the desk, legs

wide, her pert ass raised. Her fingers are between the lips of her pussy, still working her clit, but I can see she's aching now, unable to find what she needs. She's bright pink and swollen, shining with arousal, and the sight makes my dick leak precum obscenely.

"Put your fingers inside your cunt, honey."

She whimpers, a sweaty frustrated mess spread out in front of me, but she obediently slips two fingers inside her, her hips instantly resuming that frantic rocking motion.

"Does that feel good?" I stroke my hands over her still-pink ass.

She shakes her head, hissing out a breath. "No, I need more."

"You really do need my dick inside you, don't you?" Oh god, this power play is making me drunk. It's making me high. I'm on the damn brink myself, needing to press myself into her and feel her pussy strangling my cock, but watching her tremble and need, need *me*, holy shit.

"Yes, sir," she rasps out, her back undulating as she juts against her fingers, letting out more of those sweet little growls.

"Here, honey. Let me make it all better." I tease her clit with the tip of my cock, rubbing all that pre-cum all over her, and with an impatient little yelp she removes her fingers from her pussy. She braces herself on the desk on her forearms, and looks over her shoulder at me. Her lips are trembling, her hair stuck to the beads of sweat on her face. Such a pretty mess. "Is this what you need?" I slide into her, just a little, just enough to start stretching her, and her eyes roll back in her head.

"Oh, *fuck*," she murmurs.

More, and more, until her pussy has completely swallowed my cock, and she moans and sighs and says *Yes, yes,*

yes, over and over, arching her head back. When I pull out of her, just a little, my cock is slick with her juices.

"So wet, pretty girl," I murmur, running my hands down her back, over the curve of her ass, to come to rest on her hips. I thrust back inside, hard, and her fingers scratch against the surface of the desk. I've never been happier to not be the chivalrous gentleman as I am now, because her naked skin, *so* hot and wet, is a dream. "Where do you want me to come?"

She mewls again, so impatient and frustrated, and my brain misfires because she's bouncing herself back on me. I know I should stop her, I'm meant to be controlling this scene, I'm meant to be guiding her. But watching her use me like this, rubbing her needy cunt up and down my length, it's fucking incredible.

Just let it happen, just for a minute. I keep my grip on her hips, holding her steady as she thrusts back again, and again. Her back is slick with sweat, and the sounds coming from her sweet lips have changed into something carnal and strained.

"Fuck," she whimpers. "Fuck, *fuck*." She moans, loudly, and with another choked half-sob, she shakes her head. "M-more, I need more."

I hook a hand under her knee, pushing it up onto the desk, and she cries out at the depth of my intrusion. I reach around to press a hand to her lower stomach, which earns me a scream. The sound is like music, like some primal hymn that sets my blood on fire.

I fuck her hard, her pussy spasming around me as her orgasm builds. I pant against her neck, telling her she's mine, *mine, this pussy is mine,* and she moans and screams, *I'm yours, oh fuck, I'm yours,* over and over.

She sucks in a breath, going quiet, her back tensing

against my chest, and she tightens around me, so tight I see the fucking eyes of God himself. I press harder against her stomach, so she's filled with me, so full she can't breathe or speak or think, and then, she screams. Her thighs shake violently as her orgasm barrels through her, her stomach contracting under my hand. She's hard and soft all at once, hot and spent and covered in sweat.

I groan into her hair, my cock twitching, the first hot stream of my orgasm exploding inside her. With a panicked, ragged breath, I pull out, and thrust my cock between the slick cheeks of her ass, my release pooling at the small of her back. She moans softly, shaking, aftershocks wracking her body, her head tipping back against my chest.

"Theo," she whispers, and I curl my hand around her jaw, pressing kisses to her temple.

"I'm here, honey. You did so well."

"It, oh god... It was... I needed it so bad."

"I know you did." I stroke her cheek, and she tries to stand up. "Wait, honey, I made a mess of you. Let me clean you up." I yank open the drawer, but there's nothing I can use. With a grunt, I grab my sweater, because who gives a fuck. I clean her off, and she slowly puts her trembling leg down on the ground.

"Theo," she murmurs again, and turns around to face me. Her eyes are hooded, like she's drunk herself, like we both just got high on all of this and now we're both addicts. She wraps her arms around my neck, and kisses me, hot and sweet, her tongue stroking mine. I never want to let go. I could stay here forever.

"Come on, honey." I scoop her up in my arms, and she gasps, holding on as I carry her out of the office and up the stairs.

"What are we doing?" She asks, her head falling against my chest again, and it feels like the most bittersweet feeling in the world, to have her pliant and trusting in my arms.

"Now, it's time for aftercare."

———

Amber is surprised when I wash her in the shower, lathering up every inch of her, washing her hair, rinsing her down until she's fresh and clean. I rub lotion into her skin, taking special care with her tender ass. But she doesn't complain. She lets me look after her, smiling softly every time I tell her how beautiful she is, how perfect, how heavenly.

With her hair wrapped in a towel, she flops down on the bed, completely naked. Within minutes, she's asleep. I chuckle as I get dressed, and my stomach growls loudly, protesting at the lack of food I've consumed since this woman walked into my house and took over my life... Twenty-four hours ago. How has it only been 24 hours?

I consider waking her and insisting she eat too, but she looks so peaceful that I decide to leave her, and head down-stairs alone.

My phone is flashing when I get to the kitchen. I pick it up to see a few messages from Laurie, one from a colleague at work, a few from my gym buddies asking where I am, and one from my older brother. Martin and I don't talk as much as we should, but we were always close growing up. I open the message to see some pictures from his latest trip to Vietnam, and then a follow-up asking, *You free to talk?*

Suddenly, all I want to do is talk. I want to tell someone about the girl in my bed and the way she's made me feel like myself for the first time in years. I obviously can't. But if

I can just talk to someone about it, without telling them who it is...

Martin's phone rings three times, and then there's a deep, "Hello, little brother," as he answers. "How are you?"

"Hey, I hope this is a good time."

"Absolutely fine," he replies. "Just sitting here enjoying the sunshine."

"Sounds great." I tap my fingertips along the countertop. "How are you?"

"I'm really good. Just got back yesterday."

I stroll to the window, looking out at the rain that is falling heavier now, the sky dark and grey, making the yellow trees at the edge of my yard even more brilliant.

"I saw your pictures, looks like it was a great trip."

"It was. I mean, the conference was boring, but they always are." He lets out a short laugh. "Doctors, I swear, we're the most boring group of people on the planet."

"Engineers aren't much better," I reply, and turn to the fridge to take out a bottle of orange juice. "How's Joanna?"

"She's good, she's down in Florida visiting her mother. Celebrating the all-clear from cancer."

I clench my eyes shut, cursing myself for not remembering that my own brother's mother-in-law was fighting cancer for the last three years. "Shit, of course, I'm so glad to hear she's doing good."

"Hey, no it's alright, we all got our own stuff going on, right?" A screen door slams in the background, and a dog barks. "Sisco, stop." Martin snaps, and the dog complains quietly. "Good boy. So," his voice gets louder as it's clear he's talking to me again. "How are you, anyway? Enjoying the empty nest?"

"Uh, yeah, I guess." I cast a glance up at the ceiling, in

the direction of my bedroom. "I, uh, I actually... Um, met someone."

"Oh," Martin's voice brightens instantly. "That's great, do I know her?"

"No, no." I say it too fast, and clear my throat. "No, she's, uh, someone from college." *Idiot.* I clench my eyes shut, because while it's technically not a lie, I don't tell my brother that it's someone not from *my college*, and definitely not a colleague. "But, you know, it's nothing serious or anything, we're just um... Anyhow-"

"Is something wrong?" Martin interjects. "You sound... weird."

"No, I'm fine, I'm fine, I just..." I take a deep breath. What did I want? What did I even want to say to Martin about all this? "I don't know. This woman, she makes me feel like I'm some young man again, y'know?"

"Well, that's good. Just don't tell Mom, she'll be planning your wedding before you know it."

I huff out a laugh. "Yeah I don't think this girl wants to get married to me."

"Uh-oh."

My stomach drops, because I just used the word *girl* like a total idiot. "I mean-"

"You know what you sound like?"

I shake my head as though Martin could hear the metal balls rolling around inside my stupid hollow skull. "What?"

"Like when you met Mella." Martin laughs again. "I remember you calling me and saying, Oh this girl is amazing but she would never marry a schmuck like me, and then, next thing you know she's at our house and mom's asking her which one of the family rings she wants for your engagement."

"I promise you, it's nothing like that." I laugh, the

sound a little harsher than I intended. "There's... plenty of reasons why, but... I think it's more about how I feel like myself around her. In a way I haven't, y'know. In a really long time."

"And that's great. It's easy to lose yourself in the Every Day." Martin takes a sip of something, probably his morning coffee, and sighs. "Especially when we have kids. I know it's different for women, but Joanna struggled with it a lot, cutting her hair and dressing differently after Riley was born. She struggled with her own identity outside of being someone's mom, and it took her a long time to regain that because, y'know, society."

"I can only imagine how tough that would have been."

"But, even for us, at least the half decent fathers among us, we change too. And it's not easy, is it? Waking up one day to look in the mirror and see your hair's turning grey and you need glasses and you're thicker around the middle than you remember being." He chuckles softly. "I mean, maybe not for you, Mr Universe, but for the rest of us."

"Yeah yeah, I still look more like dad than I'd like to admit," I say with a laugh.

"Oh god, don't remind me. When did we all get as old as he was?" He grunts out a laugh, then exhales heavily. "Well, even if it's not super serious with this woman, I'm glad that you're having fun and finding yourself a little again. We were all worried about you for a while there."

I swallow hard, and my face feels hot. "You were?"

"Sure. After the divorce, you were so sad. For a really long time, too. And then, what was her name?"

My heart sinks, and I puff out a breath as I look down at the floor, grinding my foot into the wood. "Tanya."

"Yeah, that bitch." Martin grumbles out an insult I don't quite catch, but if he covered it after calling my ex-girlfriend a bitch, it was probably *really* bad. "You were a wreck after her. Mom nearly moved down there to be with you."

I suddenly feel funny, wobbly and dizzy, and I lean heavily against the window frame to keep myself steady. "I think it was just rebounding from Mella, and then from... Tanya." Saying her name twice in a short space of time makes my mouth sour. "But I'm fine now. Really."

"Good. That makes me happy." Martin's voice fades a little, as he talks to someone in the background. "Sorry, I'm going to have to cut this short, Jasper has baseball."

"Not a problem, tell him I said hi."

"Uncle Theo says hi," Martin says to his son, and I hear a loud *Hi Uncle Theo!* in the background. "I'll call you later, unless... you're busy?" His tone is teasing, and I roll my eyes.

"I'll call you next week."

"Oh, so you *are* busy."

I groan, and Martin laughs. "Go take your son to baseball."

"Will do! Have a great weekend!"

The line goes dead, and I stare at my phone screen for a minute. I'd had no idea my family had worried about me back then, in the years after my divorce and my relationship with that woman. I don't even want to think of her name now after saying it out loud.

Sure, they'd called more often, made excuses to come through town and see me. But I'd thought nothing of it. Because they hadn't really known the extent of what happened. How much she'd hurt me.

I gaze back at the ceiling, thinking about the woman lying in my bed, and chide myself. I always make the same mistake. I should have sent her away yesterday. And not because I didn't want to sleep with her. But because I can't separate the two things - sex and love.

It doesn't work for me. I can't be casual. I can't be short-term. I can't be someone's fuck buddy.

And now I've just sabotaged myself.

Nice work, Rembrook.

I know I should send her away. It'll hurt me, but spending the next day and a half with her will make it worse. So much worse.

I cross the hallway into my office, and pick up the soiled sweater I used to clean her up, and her lacy white panties. I stare at that scrap of material, dangling from my finger. I think about how good she felt. How much she trusted me. How eager she was to submit.

And my logic loses out.

Sending her away now will only hurt her, and betray her trust in me. I can't do that.

No, I have to see this through. I have to be who she wants me to be, who she needs me to be. I promised that to her. And whatever I feel on Monday morning, it'll be my problem to deal with.

And it won't be that bad anyhow. A few Hallmark movie marathons and too much whiskey, and I'll be fine. Love at first sight, or first fuck, that isn't real.

I'm too old to believe in all of that.

4

SATURDAY AFTERNOON

AMBER PADS down the stairs just after 2pm, and my heart takes a leap when she walks into the kitchen. She's wearing panties, and a tiny white cropped tee, the swell of her breasts just visible beneath the hem. She runs a hand through her tousled hair, and gives me coquettish smile

"Sorry, I kind of passed out," she says shyly. "You, uh, wore me out a little this morning I guess."

"I guess so." I cross the kitchen to take her in my arms, and she gazes up at me with those big brown eyes. "Are you alright? After this morning?"

She nods, biting her lip, and there's an unwelcome, comforting tug in my chest.

"Good." I kiss her forehead, and allow my hands to stray just a little, over the curve of her ass. "Can I get you something to eat? You must be hungry?"

"Ooh, yes please. I'm starving." She perches on one of the stools at the counter, tucking her hair behind her ear. She looks heavenly, as usual, half naked and tanned and delicious.

I stop staring long enough to cross the kitchen to the

fridge, pulling it open and regarding its contents. "I can make you an omelette if you like. I have spinach, mushrooms, bacon."

"Sounds great!"

I get the ingredients out of the fridge and set about cracking eggs into a bowl, chopping up the vegetables, all the while keenly aware of her watching me.

"Were you always into that kind of thing? What did we did this morning?" She asks after a while. "Y'know, BDSM, all that stuff?"

"I, uh, yeah." I shrug lightly as I keep slicing the mushrooms. "I discovered it back in college. A girlfriend of mine, she was really into spanking and choking and being tied up. She took me to a dungeon she used to go to a lot."

"A dungeon?" Amber squeaks. "Like, a sex dungeon?"

I chuckle and nod. "Yes, a sex dungeon."

She leans on the counter, and her eyes are wide when I look up again. "Did you have sex there? In front of people?"

My cheeks flush, because I haven't spoken about this in a long, long time. "I did. I, uh, was tied up to a cross once, and had the domme jerk me off and edge me for an hour, in front of a lot of watching eyes."

Amber's mouth drops open. "Theo! And here I was thinking you were some sweet engineering professor who just happened to like the gym." She giggles and shakes her head. "And now I find out you're into BDSM and sex dungeons."

I laugh as I chop the spinach and drop it into the bowl of eggs. "Look, it was a long time ago. But it did introduce me to things that I liked, and that I wanted to do with other partners. And I got a bit of a reputation at college for my... proclivities."

"Now that's a big word for sex fiend." She holds up her

hands and gives me a brilliant smile. "I'm joking, I'm joking! It's seriously kind of hot. Like, really hot."

"Yeah, but all of that kind of fell by the wayside when I got married, and then being a dad, working, all that kind of thing, you know, it just wasn't that important anymore."

I turn on the frying pan, seasoning the eggs with plenty of salt and pepper, and Amber comes to sit on the counter beside me, her long legs crossed at the ankles and swinging gently back and forth.

"So you still enjoyed vanilla sex after that?" She asks, running a hand through her hair and flipping it over her shoulder.

"Of course, I don't need it to be kinky to enjoy it."

"But if you had a partner who was into that kind of thing, would you do it more?"

I consider my answer as I fry the bacon in the pan, listening to it sizzle in the heat. "I mean, sure. If that's what she wanted. But finding people who are on the same wavelength as you isn't always easy."

"That sounded heavy." Amber raises her eyebrows as she looks at me. "Did you have a bad experience or something?"

I give her a smile, shaking my head. "Are you sure you're not psychic, Miss Pope?"

Her cheeks flush when I call her that, the slight shift in her hips telling me she really likes that nickname. "You just looked really sad when you said it."

I flip the bacon and sigh heavily, shifting on my feet as I take down a plate from the cupboard overhead. "After Mella and I divorced, I got involved with a woman I'd met at the gym. She was a little younger." I look at Amber over my glasses. "No, not as young as you."

She giggles, but doesn't say anything.

"We got on well," I go on, taking the bacon from the pan and putting it on the plate. "She was funny, smart, worked in investment banking. And after a few weeks of us sleeping together, she opened up to me about her likes and desires, and told me that she went to sex clubs in the city regularly."

"Oh, like swingers clubs?"

I smile at the term. "Swingers club always makes me think of those 70s pornos. But yes. A swingers club, I suppose. Glory holes and voyeur rooms and you name it. She asked me to go with her, and I did." I pour the eggs into the pan, and brace a hand on the counter. "It was a lot of fun, at first. After the divorce and all that, it felt good to let loose a little."

"So what went wrong?"

I stare at the eggs, setting in the pan, and try not to focus on the icy coil forming in my stomach. "We'd been dating for over a year, she'd met Laurie, they got on great, I was going to ask her to move in. It all seemed good." I trail off, folding the omelette on top of itself, and flipping it. "Then I woke up one morning, in agony. It felt like someone had my... balls in a vice."

"Oh my god." Amber's eyebrows shoot up. "What happened?"

"I went to the doctor and it turned out I had gonorrhoea."

"Holy shit!" Amber sits up straight, covering her mouth with her hands. "She gave it to you?"

I take the omelette from the pan, putting it on the plate beside the bacon, and get a knife and fork out of the drawer. Amber follows me back to the counter and sits on the stool, but she won't touch the food, her eyes still fixed on my face.

"Come on, eat." I gesture to her plate, and she shakes her head.

"What happened?"

I sigh heavily. "She'd been cheating on me. The entire time. When I confronted her, she acted completely surprised, saying it was part of the lifestyle. She said... she said that maybe I just didn't understand BDSM like I thought I did, what it was all really about."

"That's called gaslighting, and it's disgusting." Amber's voice is filled with outrage. "She never said anything to you about sleeping with other people?"

I shake my head, and am relieved when Amber finally huffs out a breath and takes up her knife and fork to start eating.

"At the club, we'd played with other couples, that was fine. But it was always talked about before, and agreed on. I had no idea she was out there, sleeping with other men, and not using protection. I thought she was just with me."

Amber gives me a sympathetic look as she chews her food, and reaches out to take my hand.

"Anyway, after a very expensive course of antibiotics I was fine. Thankfully it was easy to cure. But she was angry that I broke up with her over it."

Amber's face is pure violence. "Excuse me?"

"Yeah, she got kind of vindictive. Started telling people at the gym that I was some fiend, that I'd forced her to have hardcore sex, that I'd tied her up and hit her against her will." I hang my head as I remember the way people had started looking at me back then. "It was all kind of a mess."

"Oh shit, Theo." Amber turns in her seat and takes my hand in hers. "That's awful."

"Yeah, it was." I frown and clear my throat. "I changed gyms, never went back there. Told my dean at the college that an ex was spreading rumours about me, because I was honestly afraid I'd lose my job."

Amber sighs and shakes her head. "I am so sorry."

"It's alright. She got bored of smearing my name pretty fast, thankfully. And then, well, I guess it made me nervous." I stroke Amber's hand with the back of my fingers. "To do that again with someone. I've never wanted to hurt anybody, it was always meant to be about having fun, about bringing pleasure to each other. I've always used safe words and the traffic light system, non-verbal cues, everything to keep my partners safe. It was meant to be something I did with someone I loved." I look up at her and shrug. "Doing that with you this morning, it... It was kind of healing. To see you enjoy it so much, to have you trust me like that. It felt really good."

Amber throws her arms around my neck, pulling me over to her to kiss me, slow and deep. Without breaking the kiss, she climbs into my arms, straddling me on the stool. Her skin is warm under my hands, and having her wrapped around me like this, it's blissful.

"I loved doing that with you," she murmurs against my mouth. "I did. I felt safe, and cared for." She takes my face in her hands, and her eyes meet mine. "You're a good man. The *best* man there is. And when I walked in here yesterday, I did because I knew I could trust you. I knew you would treat me good, and look after me." She kisses me again. "I know that I'll always remember this weekend. I will. And only because you were so wonderful to me."

The words drop into my stomach like a lead weight. *Just this weekend.*

I lean my head against hers, and swallow what I want to say. Because I'm just an old fool giving a young woman a good time. That's all it ever will be. I know that.

But it hurts all over again to hear it.

I don't let myself dwell on my internal struggle for too long, because Saturday is fading away, and I'm not going to waste any more time feeling sorry for myself.

And it's easy to let all the sad, self-pitying thoughts ebb away when Amber drags me upstairs. When we end up in bed, it's not to fuck, although we're both mostly naked. She just wants to kiss. I don't know how long we lie there, but it feels like a moment I could exist in forever - the rain beating against the window, the light fading as the afternoon wears on, and Amber, warm and soft in my arms as my mouth devours hers.

"I haven't made out like this since high school," I say with a soft laugh, rolling onto my back with her, so she can straddle me.

She leans over me, pressing our bodies together, her hands under my head as she giggles against my mouth.

"I can assure you, no one I've ever made out with has been as good a kisser as you."

"Honey, you are going to inflate my ego to dangerous levels if you keep talking like that." I grip her ass, grinding my engorged cock into the heat between her legs. "Along with some other things."

"You deserve to have an inflated ego, though." She sits up, her fingers running down my chest, to my stomach, tracing the ridges of my abs. "I mean, look at you."

I tuck my hands behind my head and laugh, my cheeks burning with joy and a little embarrassment. "Yep, ego is definitely getting bigger."

She laughs, rocking her hips, and she bites her lip as I suck in a breath. "I wonder how long I'd have to do this before you come?" She gathers her hair up on top of her head with both hands, and her tee rides up to reveal more of her breasts.

"Goddamn, you look good right now." I reach over to the nightstand and grab my phone. "Stay like that."

"Theo, what are you doing?"

I grin up at her as I open the camera. "No faces, I promise. But if I don't have a picture of you like this, I'm going to be miserable for the rest of my life."

"Oh, well in that case." She stretches a little more, arching her back, and her nipples are just visible from under the ragged edge of the tee.

"Perfect." I take the picture, and turn my phone to show her. "See? No faces."

She leans in to look and giggles. "I look kinda hot."

"Not kinda, honey. Really hot. Like a goddess."

She sighs happily, her hands still in her hair as she tips her head back, rolling her hips on me slowly. "This feels so good."

It sure does. I lie back, watching her body undulate as she continues that slow rhythm. Even through my boxers and her panties, the heat is intoxicating. She goes on and on, tension growing low in my groin. It's good, so good, too good, and I wallow in it, in this feeling of wanting more but watching her just stroking herself along my length.

She lets out a whimper, her hands dropping from her hair so it tumbles down her back. She puts her hands on her breasts, massaging them and pinching her nipples, her hips rocking harder now. I feel drunk again, drunk and high, pushed to the fucking pinnacle of arousal watching this beautiful woman on top of me.

"Take off your panties," I tell her, and moving just as slowly and languidly, she climbs off me, her face dreamy and love-drunk, peeling off her panties as I shuffle off my boxers.

She climbs back on top of me, my cock pressed to my stomach by her weight, and holy hell, she's wet and dripping, heat cascading over my length as she resumes that motion, dragging her pussy along the underside of my cock.

I look down my body to where she's riding me, her rosy pink skin that's enveloping my cock, a tiny moan leaving her lips every time her clit rubs against the tip. I grab my phone again, switching the camera to video, and film that beautiful sight for 30 seconds. She watches me do it, and we're both silent - no faces, no voices, like we agreed.

Why does this feel so wrong and yet so hot?

I stop the recording, and look up at her face. She's flushed now, her cheeks a sweet shade of pink. She raises herself off me, looking down at my cock that's now practically throbbing, and she licks her lips.

"Can... Can you film when it goes in? Please?" She asks shyly, and puts her hand around the base of me.

Yeah, I fucking can.

I nod, opening up the camera to video again, and position in close as Amber lifts herself further, pressing my leaking tip to her entrance. She bites back a moan as she lowers herself onto me, and it feels filthy to film her sweet cunt stretching to take me in, inch by inch. It's hard not to shake and just lose my composure while she takes all of me. Then she's sunk down, down to the very base of my cock, soaking me, and I stop the recording, dropping the phone on the bed beside me.

Amber experiments with her movement as she stays on top of me, bouncing on me gently at first, then rolling her hips like before. She rocks them back and forth, then in an almost figure 8 motion, all the while moaning softly. She leans back, bracing her hands against my thighs, and when she rocks her hips this time, she moans loudly.

"Did that feel good, honey?" I ask, my own voice husky as arousal winds its tendrils around my ribs and my stomach. I may be tense but I'm not close to release yet, and thank fuck, because this feels incredible and I'm not ready for it to be over yet.

Amber nods, repeating the motion again, her head thrown back, her lips trembling. "O-*oh*, my god." She starts to fuck me harder now, finding that spot that has her back arching and her hands digging into my thighs. She lets out long, shaky breaths, and I still don't move even though the urge to pound up into her and chase my own release is clawing at me.

"That's my girl." I groan, looking down at where we're joined, where everything is wet and glistening, her clit full and pink. "God you look so beautiful like this, so fucking perfect for me."

She falls forward onto me with a moan, sweat lining her lips as she kisses me hungrily, panting and trembling, her hips still rolling on me.

"Y-you feel... Oh fuck, Theo." Her hips jut desperately against me. "Can we... From behind, please? Can you film us like that? I want to see it."

"You better get on all fours then."

She clambers off me, to the end of the bed, getting on to all fours like I told her to. I rise to my knees, phone in hand, and position myself behind her. I want to talk, even though we agreed not to. It feels so detached and clinical to not say anything, to not talk her through it as I crown her entrance. I bite down on my lip hard, watching through the phone screen as I sink into her, slowly, so slowly.

Liquid heat shoots through my veins as I bottom out,

and I know we agreed to be quiet but I can't help but groan. Her pussy is strangling me like this, so perfectly tight and hot. She's trembling lightly, breathing hard, her moans soft and sharp. She moves to rest on her forearms, and I nearly smash my phone in my hand, the change in angle stealing all the air from my lungs.

Her tee slides down to expose her breasts, and she's perfect, stunning. How did I end up with this girl in my bed? I grip her hip with my free hand, and begin to fuck her, every thrust a fight to get back into her even through she's so wet she's soaked my lap and my stomach. Her tits bounce with every stroke, and the sight is beyond incredible.

How the fuck did I ever forget how good this was? To just spend hours and days in bed with someone, drowning myself in the feeling of another person, in sharing pleasure with them, worshipping another body like it was the only fucking temple that would ever matter in my life? When did I forget *this*?

It's carnal, and primal, and fucking beautiful. I rock in and out of her faster, and faster, her hands gripping the sheets, her back dipping and arching as she presses her ass towards me. She lets out a strangled moan, and the next time I thrust back inside her, she jams a fist against her mouth. I can barely get back inside her as she pulses, her thighs spasming as she comes apart for me.

But I'm not done, I'm not there yet, taking a steadying breath to delay my orgasm. And I want to fucking talk.

I swipe clumsily at the screen, tapping the button again because I'm sure I missed it the first time, and dump the phone on the bed.

"You're doing so fucking good, honey," I grit out. "But I want you to give me one more."

Amber moans into the bed, protesting without words, and I run down the slope of her back, which is now damp with sweat.

"You can come for me again, can't you, pretty girl?" I thrust into her hard, and her hands spread on the bed. "Can you do that for me?"

"Theo," she pleads, and answers my question with a rock of her hips, whimpering as she squeezes herself back down my length. "More."

I dig my hands into the flesh of her ass, and pound into her. She's playing with her clit now, I can feel her fingers there where I'm slipping in and out of her, her breathing sharp and strained. Sweat is beading between us, her skin sliding against mine. My nerves are on fire, exploding beneath my skin as we both get closer.

Amber raises herself on one hand, still rubbing her soaked clit, stroking herself as I fill her cunt over and over. Her head falls back, arching her perfect body, and I thread a hand into her hair, tugging gently as she moans. My other hand finds her breast, pinching and rolling her nipple between my fingers.

"Come for me, Amber, come for me," I gasp, and it only takes a few more strokes of her fingers and my dick before she cries out, going still before her whole body shudders. Her long, loud moan fills the room as her pussy clenches my cock inside her.

The fire in my nerves turns into an inferno, and with a few more jerks of my hips, I pull out of her with a groan, jerking my soaked cock with my hand. But Amber turns around, eagerly, almost clumsily falling to the bed, and wrapping her lips around me. I roar as she sucks hard, her tongue swirling around my tip.

"Fuck, *fuck*," I gasp. "*Amber*. Oh *fuck*."

And I explode. I dig my hands into her hair, and she's swallowing, squeezing every drop of my release from me, my hips still jerking as I fuck her mouth. I slump forward, trying to catch my breath, sweat beading on the back of my neck, and on my face, and Amber releases me with a pop. She falls onto the bed, on her side, her chest pounding, her cheeks red.

I fall down in front of her, and she nestles against me, her forehead to my chest, and I wrap my arms around her.

We must fall asleep like that, because the next time I open my eyes, it's dark, and we're still entangled with each other. I kiss the top of Amber's head, and drift back off to sleep.

This is heaven.

This is bliss.

How the fuck am I meant to let this girl go?

5
SUNDAY MORNING

DAWN IS JUST BREAKING as I open my eyes, and I look down at Amber, who is still sound asleep and nestled in my arms. I want to stay in bed with her until she wakes up, but my damn arm is cramping.

Stupid old man body.

I carefully move out from under her, trying not to wake her, and grit my teeth as my muscles spasm from lying in the same position all night. I go to the bathroom, feeling rested but weirdly hungover, like I drank just a bit too much last night even though I didn't touch a drop.

My stomach grumbles loudly, hardly surprising since I haven't eaten since lunch yesterday.

Amber is stirring when I get back to the bedroom, and she stretches her arms over her head, eyes fluttering sleepily as they land on me. She smiles indulgently, and sighs.

"Good morning," she murmurs, rubbing her eyes. "We really passed out, huh?"

"Yes we did." I lean over her to plant a soft kiss on her lips. "I'll go get some coffee on, and start on breakfast."

Amber wraps her arms around my neck and moans low in her throat. "Mmmm, you're the perfect man, do you know that?" She kisses me again, and releases me with another deeply satisfied sigh. "I'll be right down."

"Take your time, honey." I pull on my sweatpants and pick up my phone before heading downstairs.

When I get to the kitchen, I flip on the light, and when I unlock my phone, the screen is lit up with notifications, most of them from Laurie.

Shit, shit, shit.

I send her a quick text, because I know she's still asleep, making some half-baked excuse about working on my thesis and ignoring my phone. My guilty conscience screams at me that everyone somehow knows what I've really been doing, that my phone has been hacked and all the videos of me fucking Amber in my bed are now doing the rounds on social media. Everyone already knows what a perverted old man I am. It's ridiculous, but paranoia will do that to you. It fucking sucks.

The coffee machine bubbles away softly as I swipe the screen on my phone to open the picture I took of Amber yesterday. There she is, straddling me, her head thrown back, that tiny cropped tee revealing just enough of her perfect tits to have my erection growing.

I go to the videos, to the one showing Amber's pink and swollen pussy swallowing my cock. My erection does more than grow, and I rub myself through the sweats with a soft groan.

Put it away and make some breakfast, you over-sexed pervert.

I plug the phone into the charger on my counter and go to the fridge to pull out the ingredients for a breakfast feast.

My stomach protests even louder now I'm actually looking at the food. I'm starving.

Soft footsteps pad into the kitchen, and I look over my shoulder to see Amber walk in. She's got to be tempting me for more, the way she walks around barely dressed. She's wearing a tiny pair of white shorts that barely cover her ass, and another cropped tee, neon pink this time, that slouches off her shoulder. Her hair is up in a messy bun on top of her head, and she looks heavenly and tousled.

"I hope you're hungry because I am cooking every egg I have in my possession," I say, dumping everything out on the counter.

"I'm so hungry," she says, perching on the counter next to me. "I guess we've definitely been burning off more calories than we've been consuming, huh?"

"That's for damn sure." I drop a kiss to her bare shoulder before setting about whisking eggs and getting the griddle hot for the bacon. "It has been a weekend."

"And we still have *all* day, and *all* night," she says playfully. "I wonder what we could get up to in that time?"

I chuckle as I place the bacon down. "Plenty, I think."

"I sure hope so." She stretches her arms out in front of her and sighs. "Got to get my fill of you before tomorrow morning."

Tomorrow morning.

I glance over my shoulder at her, at this beautiful woman with her tanned skin and brown eyes. She's pure sunshine. She's perfect. And in 24 hours I have to let her go and pretend this never happened.

"How... How do you see this working, y'know, after?" I ask carefully, not looking at her as I flip the bacon and pour the eggs into the pan. "I mean, I'll still see you, right? When you visit Laurie, I mean, obviously, not..." I trail off, feeling ridiculous, feeling like this is asking for trouble and like I'm just making a problem where there shouldn't be one.

But Amber just hops down from the counter and goes to the cupboard to get out two cups for us, and pours us both coffee. She shrugs as she gets the milk from the fridge and meets my eyes with a smile.

"It'll just be... normal. We say hi, we're friendly, and that's all." She stirs a spoon of sugar into my coffee, tapping the spoon lightly on the edge before lifting it to her mouth and licking the coffee remnants from it. "It'll only be awkward if we decide it is. And I don't think either of us is like that. We're both, y'know, chill, right?" She hands me my coffee with a bright smile. "Like we said, it's just sex. It doesn't have to mean more than that."

I take the coffee and focus on the pan and the bacon sizzling on the griddle. "You're absolutely right, honey. I just didn't want it to be uncomfortable when you come here."

She leans her head against my shoulder. "You're so sweet, Theo."

Sweet Theo. Yeah, sure I can be him. Not stupid, sentimental old Theo who's talking himself into something that isn't there.

Amber is her easy relaxed self while we eat breakfast, talking dreamily about the places she wants to go when she graduates, the buildings and bridges and cathedrals she wants to go see. She's young and hopeful, a big, bright future ahead of her, and watching her face as she talks about it is bittersweet. A reminder of everything she has ahead of her, and everything that lies behind me.

Once we're done eating our breakfast feast, we dump the dishes in the sink and forget about them, too busy kissing and touching each other, finding our way blindly up the stairs.

Of course we end up naked, in bed, with Amber nestled in my lap. She wraps her legs around my hips, sinking down onto me, kissing me the whole time, and proceeds to fuck me so slowly, so deliciously, I swear it's a fucking dream. Everything is warm, and hazy, like we're lost in a world detached from reality. My hands in her hair, her arms draped around my neck, the gasps and mingled breaths we share as we kiss for what feels like hours, make me sure I've died at some point during the weekend and actually gone to heaven.

"I could do this with you for days, I think," she murmurs, shifting her hips forward and taking me deeper. "Just... just like this. Not going anywhere, just... Just fucking you, for days."

"So could I." I gently pull her head back, nibbling at the delicate skin of her throat. "Too damn good."

"Mmmm," she hums softly, and lets out a soft giggle as I lock my arms around her waist and flip us so I'm on top of her. "Oh, *oh*, Theo."

"You lie back and let me look after you." I withdraw from her, kissing and licking my way down her naked body, all the way down to between her thighs. She sighs gently as my tongue swirls over her clit, and I lick her just as slowly, lazily, listening to every moan that falls from her lips, every small gasp as her orgasm builds.

"*Theo*," she murmurs, her fingers raking through my hair. "Oh god."

My hand skates up her body, caressing her hard nipples, rolling her breast in my hand. "I've got you, honey," I murmur against her heated skin. I lock my mouth over her again, pushing my tongue inside her, then back up over her swollen clit. She tastes too good, and I'm greedy for it, for her taste and her scent.

Her movements are still as slow and languid as they were before, her breath releasing in soft moans and small gasps. Being with this girl, it's simply intoxicating. Again, I'm drunk on her, on this feeling, on the way her skin feels against mine, the way she tastes like something I'd never had before but is somehow my favorite thing. She's soft, warm and hot, stretched out in my bed like she's been there a million times before and never belonged anywhere else.

Her breath comes faster now, her thighs trembling slightly. She's beyond soaking wet, and I drink her down, every drop, like I'm dying of thirst. Her fingers start to claw at my scalp, and she whimpers, tossing her head on the bed as her back bows away from the sheets. The chorus of her cries and moans builds, and builds, until my girl shatters. She shakes, crying out, her cunt pulsing against my mouth.

"Oh my god," she whimpers, quivering violently. "I-I... Oh." She goes soft, boneless on the bed, moaning as she tries to catch her breath.

Her pussy is ruby red with arousal, and I can't help but draw her clit back into my mouth. Amber hisses in a ragged breath, then releases it with a shaky moan.

"Theo, I'm... I'm too... *Oh*."

She's not too sensitive. Not at all. Within seconds she's running her fingers through my hair, rolling her hips against my face, her next orgasm building, and it only takes a few minutes to have her unravelling. She shakes violently this time, one hand buried in my hair and the other clutching a handful of bedsheets. She lifts her head from the bed, mouth open as she sucks in breath after breath, then drops back to the bed with a strained half-scream as the full force of her second orgasm tears through her.

And I still haven't had enough.

"Again?" She whimpers as I suck her clit back into my mouth.

Wordlessly, I rise to my knees, bringing her legs together and rolling them to the side. Amber gazes up at me, her lower lip trembling as I push my cock inside her. Her brow pinches as I fill her, and she's always tight, but like this, she's so tight my brain goes blank. I don't even know if I can fuck her, but I'm so far gone it barely takes any movement at all. Even just rutting into her tight cunt like this is enough to have me groaning within a minute.

"*Fuck,*" I mutter, and it's the only word circling my brain. *Fuck, she's so tight. Fuck, so hot. Want to come. Inside her.* But I can't, I said I wouldn't. I can't.

The pressure in my groin becomes unbearable, sweet and explosive, twisting the base of my spine until I can't do anything but groan.

Amber gasps as I pull out of her, my release pumping all over her hip. She watches with open hunger as my cum coats her skin, her eyes meeting mine as I come down from the high, the intoxication of being buried inside her for god knows how long.

I know I should clean her up, but my release has drained me of reason, or the ability to move, and I drop down onto the bed beside her. She reaches out to stroke my cheek, nestling closer into me, still breathing heavy.

I caress her shoulder, her collarbone, and when I open my eyes, she's gazing at me with an expression of tenderness, even awe. She moves closer to kiss me, and it's still slow and hazy, like being caught in a dream.

She keeps nibbling on my lips, planting small kisses all around my mouth, along my jawline, and once I regain control of my arms, I wrap them around her and gather her to my chest.

"You weren't kidding," she says breathily, giggling and stroking her fingers along my collarbone. "You really *do* love eating pussy."

"I told you." I kiss the top of her head, and she sighs. "Being down there, between your thighs, it's heaven. And I intend to do it at least twice more before tomorrow morning."

She nuzzles closer at the words, and the sigh that leaves her this time doesn't sound as content as the one before. But she doesn't say anything, just lies there in my arms, warm and soft, until she realises she's covered in cum and I drag her off to the bathroom to clean her up.

"So, twice more?" She grins up at me, pinching one eye closed at the stream of water as it cascades down the side of her face. "You're scheduling the pussy-eating now?"

"Well, you haven't sat on my face yet, and you absolutely need to do that. And besides that-" I lean in and plant a quick kiss on her lips. "I had a fun idea for us to try later."

Her eyes light up. "I like the sound of that."

"I'll make sure you have fun."

She wraps her arms around my neck, and gazes up at me. "How is any man ever going to measure up to you?"

Shit. The sinking feeling threatens to come back, grabbing at the base of my stomach, but I push it away. *No. Not again. Stop it. Don't ruin this.*

I smile down at her, running my hands through the damp strands of her hair, and shake my head. "You, my pretty girl, are going to have the whole world at your damn feet. Men will be begging to even get a second of your attention. And some day, some man is going to be the luckiest man out there, because you'll deem him good enough for you."

Her expression becomes earnest, her eyes wide and

shining, and her arms tighten around me as she nuzzles her face into the crook of my neck. I hold her hand to me, wishing I could say different things, make different promises, imagine a completely different future for her, one that might involve me. But I can't do that. I can't even hope for it.

"I was thinking," I say after a while, and she lifts her head from my shoulder. "I'd like to take you on a proper date tonight."

Her eyebrows shoot up. "A-a date?" She giggles, her cheeks flushing pink. "That's a little risky don't you think?"

"There's a nice little place about an hour away. It's very hidden, veryout of the way, and I doubt we'll see anyone we know there." I lift her up suddenly, and she shrieks, clasping on to my shoulders. "I want to take you on a proper date, just like you deserve."

"You really are the sweetest." She presses herself to my naked body, kissing me long and slow. "I wish I could keep you," she murmurs against my mouth.

And the sinking feeling threatens to come back.

6

SUNDAY AFTERNOON

THE SHRILL RINGING of the house phone startles us both. We moved downstairs to the lounge room after the shower, to lie on the couch and watch the fire, which then just devolved into another make-out session.

Just as Amber begins to moan and squirm on top of me, the damn phone has to ring.

Of course.

She settles back against the end of the couch, drawing her legs up against her chest, and watches me cross the room to scoop up the squawking phone.

"Hello?" I bark into the receiver.

"Goddammit, Dad, what is going on?" Laurie's furious voice sounds down the line, and instantly I feel ashamed. "I have been snapping and texting you all morning and you haven't responded once!"

"I-I'm sorry, peanut, I, uh..." I turn to look at Amber, who's staring determinedly out the window. "I told you, I'm working on my thesis. I'm sorry I-" I cut off and clutch the phone tighter in my hand. "Is something wrong? Are you OK?"

Laurie exhales heavily, and then sniffles, like she's crying. "I-I'm fine. I mean, nothing happened, I just..." She sucks in a shaky breath. "I wanted to talk to you, and I..." She lets out a little sob, and my heart is threatening to beat out of my chest.

"Laurie, what's happened? Is your mother alright? Did-"

"Her boyfriend proposed at dinner last night," Laurie interjects over another shaky breath. "And mom said yes."

"Oh," I reply stupidly, folding my arm over my chest and staring down at my feet. "You're not happy about it?"

"No, *no.*" Laurie puffs out a breath and makes a sound like a little growl. "God, I am such a fucking child. Why am I this upset? You and Mom have been divorced for like 7 years, it's not like I thought you two were going to get back together."

"It's a change, peanut, and it's a big one, y'know?" I turn to look at Amber, who is still gazing out the window at the leaves as they wave about in the strong wind that's sprung up. "It's someone new in your Mom's life, and an important someone. Even if you're happy for her, and you like him-"

"Arnold," she interjects with a sniffle. "His name is Arnold, and he's a dentist."

"Well, even if you like Arnold the dentist, you're allowed to feel what you feel."

"And I've been trying to call Amber, and she's not answering either, and... I just felt so alone." Laurie starts to cry in earnest, and I feel like an entire sack of shit.

"Oh, peanut, I'm sorry." I squeeze my eyes shut to stop myself being swallowed down by guilt and shame. My daughter has been dealing with all this shit alone while I've been fucking her best friend. *Grade A parenting, you fucking asshole.*

"No, it's fine," Laurie says, sniffling and clearing her throat. "I'm being such a fucking baby. It's not even a bad thing. It's great. He is really nice, he adores Mom, Grandma and Grandpa love him. And he's really nice to me."

"That matters a lot to me, y'know."

"I know," Laurie murmurs, and puffs out a breath. "It's just a lot, Dad. Everything's changing, and sometimes I get really scared. It's so dumb, I'm too old to feel this way."

I laugh gently. "My brilliant girl, I still feel that way sometimes, and I am a little older than you."

"Really?"

I look at Amber's profile, trying not to think about the storm of butterflies that springs up as she drapes herself over the couch, resting her chin on the back of her hand as she gazes over at me with those big brown eyes.

"Oh yes," I reply. "Sometimes the world feels like it's spinning away from you no matter how hard you try to stand still. Every now and then, you just have to let it take you with it, because who knows what could happen. Who you could meet."

"That's a really nice way of looking at it." She sniffles again and laughs softly. "I feel so stupid."

"You are not stupid."

"I didn't mean to scare you," she mumbles. "I'm sorry."

"No, don't apologise. Are you OK now?"

"Yeah, I am, promise." She chuckles amidst her sniffles. "I am, really. I was just in my feelings."

Someone in the distance calls her name, and there's a shuffling sound as Laurie seems to get to her feet. "I have to go, I was kind of hiding behind the garage, and now Grandma's looking for me."

"If you need to talk again, you can call me."

"I know, Daddy. I love you."

"I love you, too, peanut."

The line goes dead, and I wait for a moment with the phone to my ear before putting it back down in the cradle.

Amber's eyebrows are drawn up as I sit back down beside her.

"Is she alright?"

I nod slowly, putting my hand on Amber's thigh and caressing it with my palm. "Mella and Arnold got engaged."

"Oh!" Amber's tone is one of uncertainty, and she edges a little closer to me. "Laurie told me she liked him."

"She does," I say with a sigh. "I think she was... I guess she was a little surprised." I meet Amber's eyes and shrug. "And she felt alone. She's been trying to call us both and neither of us was answering."

"Shit," Amber mumbles, and her gaze drops from mine. "Well now I feel like a complete bitch."

"Me too. But she'll be alright. I think she's just over-whelmed with everything. Life, college, growing up, all the fun things." I give Amber a small smile. "All the things people your age grapple with."

Amber puffs out a breath. "That's for sure." She leans over and brushes a kiss against my cheek and springs to her feet. "I better go call her. Just make sure she's alright."

She springs lightly up the stairs, and a few minutes later her voice sounds in the distance, chatting animatedly with my daughter.

I slump into the couch and tip my head back against the warm leather. *Mella's getting married again.*

It doesn't bother me, not like that. She's a good person, an amazing mother, and, when it was good, she was a great partner. I've never wished her ill. Her being happy and content with a new husband makes me happy, too.

And yet, something niggles at me. Yesterday I told Amber I'd never get married again, that I was too old to start over. But this weekend has shown me that I'm not old, or past it, or ready for a retirement home.

I still feel young, young enough for things to happen for me, young enough that I still have a whole life to offer somebody else, and the added bonus being that I'm not bogged down by juvenile shit. I'm a grown man who owns his own house, has a steady job, makes great money, is evidently really good in bed, I work out-

What the fuck are you trying to talk yourself into here, old man?

My reason jumps up and punches me in the face like a goddamn asshole.

I'm trying to tell myself I'm an attractive prospect for Amber. Even the term makes me roll my eyes at myself. *Attractive Prospect.* I'm already talking like a goddamn fossil.

Another thing to shove down into the dark along with my shame and guilt, and all the damn butterflies that won't stop crowding my stomach. There's nothing I can say to myself that will make a relationship with Amber acceptable. Nothing will ever rationalise asking a young woman like her to give up her future to spend it with someone as old as me.

Nothing.

It's just for the weekend. And she can't keep me. We both know that.

———

Amber watches me carefully as I do the dishes, one leg drawn up to her chest, the other dangling from the kitchen counter. I give her a side glance a few times, but her eyes stay fixed on my hands in the soapy water.

Finally, I turn to her, drying my hands on a towel, raising my eyebrows.

"Penny for your thoughts?"

Her eyes snap up to mine, a smile taking over her face, and she shakes her head.

"Oh, nothing serious. Just... thinking about random things."

"What *things*?"

She suppresses a laugh, and brushes a stray strand of hair from her forehead. "I guess, it feels kinda stupid to say it, but I feel... different. I don't know how to explain it. I mean, it's just sex, right? That shouldn't make me feel different, should it?"

"I guess it depends on how good the sex is," I say with a shrug, and she rolls her eyes.

"Yeah, yeah, you're great. Life-changing. The best I've ever had."

I puff out my chest and toss the towel to the counter. "There goes my ego again."

Amber giggles as I press a kiss to her cheek, running my hands under her shirt to cup her breasts.

"It's not the sex, honey. It's you." I pinch and roll her nipples between my fingers, and she gazes up at me with hooded eyes. "You wanted to feel more confident, and you do. More confident to know how to ask for what you want, how to say yes, how to say no, all of that. Knowing your worth is important."

"And all I needed was for you to rail me all weekend to find that, huh?"

I pinch her nipples harder, and she gasps. "I think that's exactly what you were hoping for when you walked over here with no panties on."

She smiles that lecherous smile, her head tipping back as I continue to massage her breasts, her nipples hardening between my fingers. She braces her hands against the counter, her eyes closed.

"I guess it was," she murmurs, and moans softly. Her thighs open for me, and she rocks against my growing erection gently. After a few minutes, we're both hot and eager, and she tries to shuffle off her shorts.

"Wait," I say with a laugh, pulling back from her as I try to catch my breath. "We're getting all distracted when we had some things we wanted to do today, right?"

"Oh yes, your little game," Amber says, running her hands down my chest. "Let's hear it then."

I brush a kiss against her lips. "I want you to go into my office, and get undressed. Then I want you to bend over my desk, and wait there for me."

Her eyes light up and she nods. "Yes, sir." She slides down off the counter, and obediently walks from the kitchen out into the hall.

I take a deep, steadying breath. *Stick to the plan. Don't get distracted and caught up in the moment. That'll make it worse.*

Coming from the genius who just said he wanted to woo her with a proper date, it seems like I'm real bad at taking my own advice.

I square my shoulders, and put on the persona from yesterday. I'm going to make sure this last day is special for her. This isn't about me, it never was. It's about Amber, and I'm a means to an end.

I wish I could keep you. I growl out a breath. *Stop it.* I head upstairs, opening her duffle bag and retrieving the vibrator she brought with her on Friday.

In my office, Amber is obediently bent over my desk naked, her hands flat on the surface, her ass pointed at the door. She doesn't move at all when I walk in.

"You follow instructions so well, Miss Pope."

"Thank you, sir."

I round the desk and run my fingertips along its surface, placing the vibrator down right in front of her.

"Now, I'm told you made some videos, Miss Pope. The kind you'd hate for anyone to see, is that right?"

Her ribcage sucks in, and she exhales shakily, settling into the game, her shoulders relaxing. "Oh, sir, that would… I would be ruined if anyone ever saw me doing those dirty things with my *professor*."

Holy shit, she is glorious. She understands the game so perfectly, and it feels so filthy for this to be the game we choose. But we choose it anyway. If what we're doing is wrong, we may as well lean right on into it.

I take my phone from my pocket, bringing up the video of Amber rubbing her pussy along the length of my cock. I lay the phone down underneath her, right in her line of vision.

"Videos like this, Miss Pope?" I wait until the video stops, reaching down to swipe to the one of her lowering herself onto me. I tut softly, and she squirms as she rubs her thighs together. "I'm shocked, Miss Pope. I thought you were such a good girl, and here you are, riding your professor's cock?"

"I-I'm sorry, sir," she says breathily.

"Did you like it, Miss Pope?" I lean on my rolled fists, over her, my erection tenting my pants. "Did you like having that thick cock inside your wet little pussy?"

"I did, sir." She sucks in a small breath as the video loops and she watches herself slide back down onto me. "I liked it so much. I'm so ashamed."

"Does watching this video turn you on, Miss Pope?"

She nods, still holding her position over the desk. "Yes, sir."

"Show me."

She hesitates, then lifts one hand from the desk. She puts it down between her legs, moving it between her thighs once, twice, before lifting it so I can see her glistening fingers. I lean forward to take them in my mouth, licking her arousal from them.

"So wet, Miss Pope. Almost like your pussy wants a cock inside it again." I swipe to the next video, where I took her from behind. "Look how greedy you are, bouncing back on him like that."

"He feels so good, sir." She puts the fingers I just licked into her own mouth, and sucks with an appreciative hum.

"Did you let him fill your pussy with cum?"

She shakes her head, pulling her fingers from her mouth. "He won't do that, sir."

"But you want him to, don't you?" Jesus Christ, why am I playing into this part of the game?

Amber nods. "I want him to, so badly. I want to feel him running out of me."

"Such filthy thoughts, Miss Pope." I pick up the vibrator, pressing the small button near the base until it starts to buzz softly in my hand. "I'm going to have to punish you for them."

"Of course, sir."

Her submission makes my dick even harder. She's too damn perfect. Her breathing picks up as I move behind her, taking in her long legs and her pink, dripping pussy.

"Now, remember your safe word, Miss Pope."

"Yes, sir."

I touch the vibrator to her labia, and she sucks in a breath. "What is it?"

"Bridge, sir."

"Very good." I can't help but grin as I press the head of the vibrator to her entrance, and she whimpers. "Have you ever squirted, Miss Pope?"

She shakes her head, her toes curling as the vibrator circles her clit. "I don't think I can," she murmurs.

"We'll see about that." I hold the vibrator to her clit, and hit the button until it's set to an intermittent buzzing cycle, three vibrations then a pause. I run my hand up and down Amber's back as she tenses through the cycle, exhaling with every pause. "Is this how it feels when you're riding his cock, Miss Pope?"

Amber shakes her head. "No," she says, her voice more of a breathy squeak now, and she exhales in a loud *Ahhhh* when the vibe pauses. "No, it feels so much better, sir. He's so big, and hot, and when he pounds his thick cock inside me, I feel like he's going to break me in the best way."

Jesus. H. Shitting. Christ. I'm meant to be maintaining control here, but she's talking like a porn star and my dick is leaking so much pre-cum in my sweatpants that they're starting to stain. I take a deep breath, and push the vibrator inside her. She lets out a choked moan, her arms buckling a little as she presses herself to the desk.

"I'm sure you do, Miss Pope." I look down at where the vibe is inside her, coated in her arousal.

"Do you like watching me like this, sir?" She's looking over her shoulder at me, her pink lips parted as she pants, and she lifts an eyebrow.

Brat. Spectacular, sexy fucking brat.

Her eyes slam shut and she bites her lip with a hitched breath as I press the vibrator deep inside her.

"I love watching you be punished, Miss Pope." I pull the vibrator from her pussy, and her frustrated mewl is quickly covered by a loud moan as it's pressed to her throbbing clit. "How many times do you think you can come for me? How many would be a suitable punishment?"

"Thr-*threee*," she moans, her hands spread on the desk, and with a jerk of her hips she orgasms, her body shaking gently, her thighs trembling as every muscle in those perfect legs tenses.

"Only three?" I sink to my knees, turning off the vibrator. "We'll see, won't we, Miss Pope. Now, keep watching that video."

She lets out a sharp hiss as I bury my face in her still quivering cunt. Holy shit, she tastes so good, so sweet now her orgasm has soaked her. I yank down my pants, freeing my cock, fisting myself but not wanting to stroke too hard while I lick her. Goddammit, I need to relieve some of this damn tension.

She shakes and squirms and cries out, and her next climax shatters through her faster than I expected. Feeling the pulse of her hot pussy against my tongue is heaven, but even before she's stopped shaking, she's rocking her hips against my face.

"More," she moans, her breathing rapid. "Oh my god, more, please."

The pleading sends me over the edge, and I rise to my feet, kicking her legs apart and shoving my cock inside her with a moan. I thrust into her, and her ass bounces back against me, meeting me halfway each time. My hand slides up her neck, into the wild tangle of copper hair, and I wind it around my fingers, pulling her up against me so I can nip at her shoulder.

"You like having your pussy destroyed like this, Miss Pope?" I nibble on her ear lobe, and she whimpers.

"Yes, sir," she says, nodding her head against my shoulder.

"Pick up the phone," I order, and she does so with shaky hands. "Turn on the camera."

She's trying to focus and maintain control, and it takes her a second, but she opens the camera, her trembling finger hitting the arrows to spin around to the front camera.

"Now, film my cock ruining your cunt, Miss Pope."

No face, no names, no talking, that's what we said. But my reason isn't just gone, it's dead, buried somewhere in my psyche. Amber hits record, lowering the phone, and I hook a hand under her knee to open her up. She gasps, trying to stay steady, swallowing down her moans that sound as sweet whimpers in her throat.

"Whenever you want to let some useless college boy fuck you, Miss Pope, watch this video, do you understand?" I breathe against her ear. "Ask yourself if he can fill this pussy as good as I can."

Too much, too fucking much. No, it's just the game, the game, the game.

"Yes, sir." Her voice is strained and soft, one hand holding the phone and the other curled back to clasp around my neck, holding herself steady. She's playing the game too, playing right into my twisted little fantasy where I ruin her for any other man, where no one can ever compare to me, to the way I make her feel, to the way I make her come. The way I make her *scream.*

I put my other hand between her legs, spreading the

lips of her cunt, circling her swollen clit, and she slams her head back against my shoulder.

"Theo," she whimpers, the phone slipping from her fingers and hitting the ground with a thud.

"Leave it," I growl, and pound into her, stroking her clit. Both her hands are curled behind my neck now, her sharp fingertips digging into my skin. Her back arches, she becomes tighter and tighter, sweat running down her spine and pooling between us.

"Fuck, Theo, I'm going to-" She gasps, and then her pussy clenches my cock in a vice grip, her scream filling my office and the fucking cavern of my soul.

"Amber," I groan into her hair. "Amber, *fuck*."

I don't pull out in time, my release crashing through me like a Mac truck. Two pulses of my cock send hot jets of my cum into her pussy, and with an agonised moan, I grit my teeth and pull out of her. I rub my cock between her legs, the remainder of my release lashing the desk, the floor, and very probably my phone.

Amber collapses onto the desk, her arms outstretched, trying to catch her breath. I run my hands along the divots of her spine, over the beads of sweat coating her golden skin.

"You did so well, honey," I murmur, and she sighs. "You did so fucking well. You're incredible. You're a dream."

She turns around and perches on the edge of the desk, her chest still pounding. "You came inside me, didn't you?" She grins as she looks down, and my cock threatens to harden all over again as she clenches her pussy to wring the drops of my release from her. She looks up at me, triumphant, and slides two of her fingers inside her, before putting them in her mouth, drawing them between her lips with a moan.

I'm going to pass out. I'm going to fucking collapse right here, I'm a fucking old man who's at the risky age for heart attacks, right? Especially when a woman with a body like sin who is half my fucking age is here, tasting the cum I left inside her from her fingers.

"We taste even better together," she says.

I crush her against me, kissing her with a hunger and fever unlike any I've ever felt before.

She's perfect. Too fucking perfect. She'd be perfect for me. Perfect. Perfect. But no. No, not for me.

7
SUNDAY NIGHT

"How do I look?" Amber tosses her hair over her shoulder and purses her lips. She's wearing a slinky black slip dress and no bra (thank you, God), her hair curled and her cheeks glowing with some sparkly, bronze rouge.

"You look like you belong on the cover of Vogue," I tell her, putting an arm around her waist and kissing her.

She hums softly against my lips, and smiles widely. "You smell so good," she says, putting her nose to my jawline and inhaling. "Oh my god, this is like-" She sniffs again and sighs. "Like the ultimate sexy man smell."

"Well, thank you, honey." I dip my face into the crook of her neck and nip at her skin, and she shrieks, her hands sinking into my hair with a laugh.

"Your beard!" She keeps laughing as I pull back, and quickly leans in to press another kiss to my mouth. "It's so tickly."

I run a hand over my stubble that isn't really stubble anymore, and balk for a second. "I probably should have shaved, you look so gorgeous and here I am looking like a lumberjack."

"No," she says, shaking her head and draping an arm around my neck, stroking her hand along my jaw. "I like it like this."

"I'll leave it then." I kiss her forehead, and grab my glasses from the side table, slipping them on before retrieving our coats from the hooks on the wall. I help Amber into hers, and the way she tilts her head as I help her into it shows off the graceful length of her neck. I can't help leaning in to plant another kiss there, which earns me a soft little laugh.

Thankfully it's dark now, real dark, and we're once again sneaking out to my car like delinquents. Amber casts a lecherous grin into the back seat, sticking her tongue out as she turns back to me.

"Maybe we'll need to take the backseat for a spin again tonight?" She says with a laugh.

I leave her in charge of the music selection as we drive along the dark streets, and she introduces me to her favourite songs, talks about concerts she wants to go to, her hand on my thigh the whole time. Every now and then I'll wrap my hand around hers, and she snuggles into my shoulder.

It feels so nice.

Too nice.

When we reach the restaurant, the parking lot is barely occupied, and I don't recognise any of the cars here. Fairy lights hang in the trees, illuminating the coloured leaves, the porch of the rustic building decorated with flickering lanterns.

"This is so cute!" Amber's eyes are lit up with delight as I open her door for her. "It looks like something out of a fairytale!"

"It's very nice, very private, and the food is amazing." I

slip an arm around her waist as we head inside, where a friendly waitress greets us with a big smile. I'm paranoid, looking for a hint of judgement in her face, but there isn't one. I scan the other faces nonchalantly as we are led to our table, and there's no one I know, not even anyone I faintly recognize.

Amber clearly doesn't see anyone either, because she remains relaxed in my arm, smiling up at me. She's even more magical in this light, soft and glowing like she's lit from within.

"Here we are," the waitress says as we reach a table at the back by a large window overlooking a garden flecked with lights. "Now, would you like any drinks to start?"

"Do you have Dr Pepper?" Amber asks, and my stomach does another one of those stupid flips. Of course she can't drink anything stronger than that, because she's not even 21 years old yet.

The waitress doesn't miss a beat, and nods. "We sure do. And for you?" Her gaze lands on me, and I hastily clear my throat.

"Oh, uh, I'm driving, so I'll be responsible and have a Dr Pepper, too."

"Not a problem, I'll bring those right on over and take your food orders."

Amber smiles at me indulgently as the waitress leaves, and reaches across the table to take my hands. "You can start breathing again now."

"What?"

She giggles, shaking her head. "You looked so damn guilty when we walked in here, and just now, with the drinks order?" She lifts a hand to stroke my cheek. "Stop it," she murmurs, and runs a thumb across my lower lip. "I'm so happy I'm here with you. *And* I will have you know you are the most handsome man in this restaurant. Trust me. I checked."

My cheeks flush with heat, and I can't help but smile, taking her hand and pressing it to my lips. "And you are without a doubt the most beautiful woman here."

"Mmm, I don't know." Amber's lips twitch pensively and she looks in the direction of our waitress. "She really makes that outfit work." She turns back to me with a grin when I chuckle. "Come on, she's cute."

"She is, she is."

Amber tilts her head, sweeping her hair over her shoulder, and looking down at the menu. "Now, I am starving because all I ate today was some omelette and some cum, so-" She gives me a devilish grin when I choke out a laugh, and bites her thumb nail between her teeth. "I mean it is true."

"In that case you probably should eat a steak, give you your strength for tonight."

"Ooh, that sounds like a promise," she says, her eyes lighting up.

"I guess I've been doing a pretty bad job of looking after you, huh? Not feeding you right. I should work on that."

She reaches for my hand again, and shakes her head. "No, you've been doing a really good job of looking after me. So good that I don't think any man is ever going to measure up to you."

My heart does a wobbly leap, and in that moment the waitress returns with our drinks. We give up our orders - Amber does decide on a steak, which makes me smile - and once the waitress leaves, Amber eyes me from over her drink as she puts the straw in her mouth.

"This is probably the nicest date I've ever been on," she says with a coy smile.

"Where do young men take their dates these days?" I huff out a laugh. "I guess they don't take y'all to the drive-in theatre anymore?"

Amber giggles. "You know, those are actually making a comeback."

"Oh, well, everything that was once old will be new again."

Amber rolls her eyes. "And there you are calling yourself old again."

I throw my hands up in defeat. "You're right, I promised to stop. But you know, I didn't pick you up from your house or buy you flowers, so is it *really* a date?"

"I guess you could always send me flowers some other time," she says, resting her chin on the back of her hand.

"I'd need to know your favorites first."

She laughs softly, and runs her hand through her hair. "Well you can't send me those. They don't sell my favorite flowers in stores. Tulips are nice, I like those two-tone ones."

I reach across the table to take her hand. "Hold on, what are your favorites though?"

"It's kind of silly." Her cheeks flush a little pinker. "My grandparents live upstate, and behind their house there's all these orchards, acres and acres of apple and cherry trees. We used to go there for spring break when I was a kid, and the fields would all be in bloom, like a sea of white and pink." She shrugs, taking up her glass in her manicured fingers. "Apple and cherry blossoms were always my favourites. I still try to go up there in the springtime, it always makes me happy."

"That sounds beautiful, honey."

She nods, taking a sip through her straw.

"So," she says after she swallows. "You said some pretty intense things over the past couple days."

Unease instantly settles on my shoulders, and my cheeks burn with shame. "Amber, I, uh, I wanted to apologise for-"

"I'm going to stop you there." She gives me a soft smile. "I wasn't saying it because it was bad. I would have told you if it made me uncomfortable."

"It... it didn't?"

She shakes her head slowly, her eyes dropping to my hands as she reaches for them. "I, uh, I wasn't expecting this, I mean, *this*." Her eyes widen for a moment as she says it, and now her cheeks are burning bright red. I realise Amber is nervous. "I liked you, obviously, and had a stupid crush, but... I never expected it to... feel like more?"

The question hangs at the end of that sentence, and her eyes rise to mine. My stupid old brain takes a beat to realise what those words and this look mean. What she's telling me. What she's asking me.

Amber wants more.

More of me, of us, of all of this, and I hate myself for the way my heart starts to rattle at my ribcage like it wants to jump straight out of my throat and into her hands. Because yes, I want more too, I want her forever, I want her in my house and in my bed and sitting beside me in the car singing along to her favourite songs until I die.

But I can't. *Because* I want more, I can't. I fucked up. I thought it was just my heart on the line here, that my own stupidity had led me into an entanglement that would have me mournfully watching stupid Hallmark movies while drinking too much whiskey for a few weeks. I'd feel sorry for myself, sure. I'd get over it eventually.

But Amber, *Amber*? I can't break her heart. I can't do

that to her. I can't send her off tomorrow with regret and tears.

Shit. No no no, bad, BAD. Shut it down, Rembrook, fucking GENTLY.

I force my face into an understanding smile, and stroke my thumb over her knuckles. "I know what you mean, honey. I think, when you experience a kind of dom/sub dynamic for the first time, and it feels good and safe, it's normal for that to be quite intense."

She nods, taking another sip of her drink. "That makes sense."

"The talk, the dirty talk, the possessive talk, it's all part of, I guess, my thing." I jerk my shoulders into a little shrug. "Part of the scene, you know?"

"Mhmm." Amber licks her lips. "Yeah, it's all, like, roleplay?"

"Kind of, yeah. I mean, yes exactly that."

Her mouth shifts into a crooked smile. "You've always been into role-play?"

"No, just with you."

"Hmm, I like that." Her eyebrows twitch together pensively. "Is it always that way? Different things with different people?"

I pretend to be thinking as I huff out a breath, but really I'm relieved that we've changed the subject and I try to tell myself that maybe, just maybe, I was imagining everything.

"It definitely depends on the dynamic, different people obviously have different kinks and fetishes, so you work with that." I'm blabbering, my brain still running on emergency mode, trying to steer the conversation any which way but back to Amber's question of *more*. "I think we both enjoyed playing these roles. You like being possessed, it makes you feel safe, it makes you feel-"

"Loved?" She interjects, and my heart plummets straight out of my ass and into the damn floor. Her brown eyes are gazing intently at me, and she raises her eyebrows. "That's good, right? To feel love in a situation like that?"

She said love that time, not loved. I can't decide if it matters. I can't decide anything, because her eyes are staring straight into my soul like they did right before the first time I kissed her. I know now that was a mistake. This whole weekend was a beautiful, catastrophic mistake, and I don't know how to fix it.

"Feeling cared for and feeling loved are... They're very, uh, similar." God, now I'm stuttering. "And yes, in that situation, you want it to feel like, you know, you want it to feel..." *Well, what the fuck do you want it to feel like, you useless asshole?*

Amber clutches my hands tighter and shakes her head. "I've made it weird, haven't I?" She wrinkles her nose. "I'm sorry, I didn't mean for this to be awkward. I just wanted you to know that no man has ever made me feel the way you do, and that's good. That's what I wanted, right? So, you know, mission accomplished."

"You didn't make it weird, honey. I think I did." I try to laugh and sound lighthearted, holding on to her long fingers. "I don't want to hurt you. I would never want to hurt you. And I would never want you to feel that I had let you down, or that I had used you."

"I thought we established I like being used," she says with a sly grin, and I feel heat again but not in my damn face, no, in my fucking groin that still isn't getting the idea that this is a serious discussion and getting turned on right now is *bad*.

"Yes, we did," I say with a breathless chuckle. "I mean, in a way you don't want to be. I would never do that to you."

"I know that." Her eyes are still on my face when I feel something rubbing along my thigh.

Amber's foot is rubbing along my thigh under the table. That panic/pleasure combination seizes my brain again, and I don't know that anything I say right now is going to diffuse the situation. I should just shut up, and change the subject. This isn't going to get any better in a restaurant where there are other people.

Mercifully at that moment our food arrives, and Amber's foot drops from my thigh. I mumble some thanks to the waitress, my mouth just as useless as my brain, and Amber smiles at her brightly, completely nonplussed while I'm the bumbling fool across from her.

"This looks so good," Amber says, inhaling deeply over her plate. "I'm starved."

"Me, too." I'm grateful for the couple of minutes of silence as we eat to try and gather my thoughts. Am I overthinking this? Am I reading something into this that isn't there? I want to ask her for clarification, but then I'm really risking fucking things up, and actually making this into a problem. *Just calm down, Rembrook. Let her lead this conversation. Don't make things worse.*

"So, what do you have planned for the rest of our evening?" Amber's voice breaks through my thoughts, and I look up to see her smiling at me.

Exactly. Just relax. Enjoy the night. Stop overthinking.

"Aside from taking you home and showing you a good time?" I ask with a grin, and she covers a giggle.

"I thought that was obvious." She flicks her hair back, artfully sending the strap of her dress loose down her shoulder. "I was wondering if there were any specifics, *sir.*"

I'm not going to survive this meal. With a laugh, I put my hand on the table and look over at her.

"Are you wearing panties, Miss Pope?" I ask in a low voice, and her eyes sparkle.

"Yes, sir."

"I want you to go to the bathroom and take them off," I tell her. "I want you to put them in your purse and bring them to me, and then I want you to sit down and finish your meal. Do you understand?"

She nods, plucking her purse from her chair.

"What's that?" I ask, raising an eyebrow.

Amber sweeps from her chair, leaning over me, the loose strap of her dress allowing it to fall open enough for me to see her breast. "Yes, sir," she murmurs against my ear, sweeping up the strap of her dress as she stands, and makes her way across the restaurant to the bathroom.

If this is our last night, then we're going to enjoy it.

She returns after a few minutes, sashaying towards me, letting me know her ass is bare under her dress, and it feels like yet another delicious, filthy secret. A few men in the restaurant turn to watch her as she passes, their open admiration making my cock swell even more. Yes, she's beautiful, she's gorgeous, she has a body to die for, and I get to take her home and fuck her til she's screaming *my* name. *I'm a fucking caveman.*

She slides into her chair, and clicks open her purse. Under the table, she passes me something scant and lacy. I pass my fingers over the fabric before tucking it into my pocket, and tut quietly.

"Your panties are so damp, Miss Pope. Are you turned on?"

"I think I am, sir." She bites her lip, and picks up her cutlery. "I watched one of those naughty videos I made with my professor while I was in the bathroom, and it made my pussy so wet."

I am so fucking glad we're well away from anyone else in the restaurant so they can't hear us acting like sex-crazed deviants.

"You should eat, like I told you to, Miss Pope," I say, and even my voice can't hide just how aroused I am.

Amber demurely finishes her meal, and I try to do the same. Damn that hour drive home. It's so fucking far.

The waitress comes and asks if we want dessert, to which we both say no. I give the waitress an overly generous tip and pull on my coat before we cross the restaurant to cover the bulge in my pants. Amber lets me slip an arm around her waist as we walk out, and she smiles sweetly at me as I open the door for her.

"Thank you, sir," she says in a husky voice, and walks out into the crisp air.

The parking lot is quiet as we cross it, no sound but the wind whispering through the leaves, and I thread my fingers through Amber's.

"It's so cold tonight," she says, snuggling against my arm. "I'm definitely going to need warming up."

In the car, I gun the engine, and we weave our way through the dark streets back towards the highway.

"Pull up your dress," I say to her, and see her head snap in my direction out of the corner of my eye. "Your dress, Miss Pope, pull it up around your waist so your cunt is bare."

I can practically feel the smile roll off her, and she spreads her legs, the fabric of her silk black dress swishing as she shimmies it up her thighs. Once it's up around her hips, she leans back in her seat, gazing over at me.

"Like this, sir?"

I glance over, and my cock hardens ridiculously at the sight of her spread out like this next to me.

"That's perfect, Miss Pope."

"Do you want to touch?" She asks, stroking her fingertips along my arm. "Or do you want me to?"

"I want you to keep your hands away from that pussy, do you understand?"

"Yes, sir,"she purrs, and her hand drops to my crotch, feathering over my rock-hard dick. "Do you need something, sir?"

I grit my teeth as we turn onto the highway, definitely skirting the edges of the law with my speed. I curse the endless blacktop stretching out in front of me, but I also want her squirming and aching for me by the time we get home. I don't intend on sleeping much tonight.

"Get your tits out of that dress," I growl, and her sharp intake of breath betrays her surprise. I glance over at her, gauging her reaction for fear or dismay, but she just looks lustful and sinful and holy fuck I want that cunt in my face right now.

She peels the straps from her shoulders and pushes the fabric below her tits. "Like this, sir?" She suppresses a squeak as I reach over and pinch her nipple hard.

"Perfect." I put my hands back on the steering wheel, breathing through my own desire. "Tell me which video you watched."

"The one where you're-where my professor is fucking me from behind." She slips so easily back into our little role-play.

"And did it make your pussy wet, watching him put his dick inside you?"

"Yes." Her hands stray along her thighs, and she moans softly. "I wanted to touch myself."

"And did you?"

"No," she breathes, "But I wanted him to follow me to the bathroom. I had a fantasy."

"Tell me about your fantasy, Miss Pope."

She lets out a ragged breath, shifting in her seat, spreading her legs even more. "That he came in after me, and he didn't lock the door. He bent me over the counter, and gagged me with my panties, telling me I had to be quiet."

"And what did he do then?"

She breathes out, her fingers brushing over the gear shift. "He pulled up my dress, and I heard a zip, and he spat in his hand so his dick was wet. Then he told me I had to watch him in the mirror."

Just hearing this fantasy playing out in the car has me cursing myself for not thinking of it myself. I want to free my cock from my pants and stroke myself while she tells me this story, but I force myself to wait. It's not that much further, not really.

But every mile feels like an eternity.

"I kept my eyes on his face," Amber goes on. "And the way he looked when he was finally inside me, the sounds he made." Her back arches away from the seat, and she moans. "And then he whispered in my ear that he wasn't going to be gentle, that he was going to fuck me hard."

"And did he?"

She nods, running her hands along her thighs. "Yes. I could barely breathe. My whole body was on fire. I tried to stay quiet, because I knew the door was unlocked. I knew someone could walk in at any moment."

"What if someone had walked in, Miss Pope?" I glance over at her, and she gives me a crooked smile. "Or does the idea of having someone walking in on you with a dick buried inside your cunt make you even wetter?"

"Maybe it does." She stretches in her seat, kicking off her stilettos and bracing her elegant feet against the dash. "Maybe I'd like my professor to take me to a sex club, one where people could watch us."

Holy fucking god. Sweat breaks out on the back of my neck and I don't think I can make it the whole ride home. If she keeps talking like this I'm going to embarrass the fuck out of myself and come in my pants.

"Why do you want people to watch you, Miss Pope?"

She cups her breasts with a sigh, rolling her nipples between her fingers. "So everyone would know I was his, sir."

"And you are his, aren't you?"

It's just a game. Just a game. But not even the role-play can remove the possessive stab of jealousy in my chest, because dammit she *is* mine.

"Yes, I am, sir," she says softly, her head tipping back as she keeps playing with her tits. "All I can think about is him being inside me, the way it felt when he lost control and came inside me, it made me feel like I only ever want to be his."

This isn't feeling like a game.

I want to pull over and fuck her now, in the car. She's starting to squirm in her seat, and I know she's needy, as needy as I am. The quiet highway streaks past us as I speed towards our house.

"How did your fantasy end, Miss Pope?" My voice is

gravelly, my grip on the steering wheel is like iron, and I'm trying like hell to steer the conversation back to the game, the fantasy, not the very real desire to spank Amber until her ass is raw, then fuck her until every hole is full of me and she never leaves my bed again.

Caveman. Fucking insane caveman.

"I came so quick," Amber says, and her voice is more like a moan now, a breathy, needy moan as she squeezes her nipples. "Because he was so big, and he fucked me so hard. But he didn't stop, even when I was clawing at the mirror, he kept fucking me, and telling me that I was his dirty little slut, just his, to fuck whenever and wherever he wanted."

Where can I pull over? Fuck, I need to pull over now.

"And then he came." Amber undoes her seatbelt and kneels on her seat, reaching over to undo my pants, and frees my cock, feathering her fingers up and down my length. "He pumped me so full of cum, it was running down my legs."

Fuck. Goddamn. Are we nearly home? We have to nearly be home.

"Keep driving," Amber murmurs, and I expect her to give me head, or jerk me off til I explode all over the steering wheel. But she pumps me gently, running her thumb over my tip to collect the pre-cum that won't stop leaking, and does nothing more. "I want you to take me to a club," she whispers in my ear. "I want you to sit back and watch other men fuck me, but only because you say they can. I want to be tied down and blindfolded, and be used while you watch. And then I want you to fuck me. In my pussy, my mouth, even in my ass if you want, because I'm yours and you can do what you want to me."

I swallow down my groan. "You want to be shared with other men?"

"I want to be used, Theo." She presses her hot lips to my neck. "I want to be fucked and used like a doll, I want you to fuck my mouth til I choke. I want my pussy to be so sore I can't walk. Because you did it to me, and I wanted you to." She licks my skin, and I can't suppress this groan anymore, my cock swelling and twitching in her hand. "I want to be yours, Theo. Your dirty little slut. Can I be that for you?"

A serrated breath bursts from my lungs as I take the exit towards home. I wrap my hand around Amber's, stilling her movements but lifting my hips to grind myself against her palm.

"You're my dirty little slut," I say, and she smiles against my skin. "And when we get home, you're to go inside, take off this dress, and go to my room. Get on your knees, and wait for me there."

"Yes sir," She snuggles against my shoulder, continuing to stroke my dick, until we pull into the driveway of my house. The street is dark, and quiet, and Amber adjusts her dress before I open her door. She takes off her stilettos and tiptoes silently across the driveway.

I stride after her and unlock the door. But once we're inside, when Amber moves to obey me, I grab her arm and spin her against the wall. Her big eyes gaze up at me, her breath coming heavy.

The door falls closed, and I want to keep playing this game, I want to maintain control. I'm the dominant here, right? I should be able to keep the scene going.

But I fucking can't.

"I should be better at this," I murmur, threading a hand into her hair. "I should be, shouldn't I?"

The corners of her mouth tug into a grin. "Better at

what? Being the big man?" She cranes her neck, to nip at my lips with her own. "You think that's all I want from you? The dom?"

Our breath is mingling, our lips brushing but not completely touching.

"Isn't it?"

She shakes her head, pulling me closer so her body is pressed between mine and the wall, the streetlight falling through the frosted glass of the door, illuminating her eyes.

"You think I don't want you to lose control?" She grinds her hips against me, and a shuddering groan reverberates through my throat. "I do, Theo. Whatever you have to give me, I'll take it."

She didn't call me sir that time. This isn't a game.

The dangerous, hopeful, painful thought that this is real is intoxicating. There's no space between us, only heat, and electricity, the pounding heart that's so loud I swear it takes up all the space in my brain, until there's nothing but her and the warmth of her skin and the cotton candy scent of her hair.

And I lose control.

Amber moans into my mouth as I crush hers, lifting her up so her legs can lock around my hips. The silky black dress rides up her thighs, my hands digging into her ass as her teeth clamp down on my lower lip. She's tearing at my shirt, and buttons ping to the ground one after another. She moves lower, to my pants, freeing my aching cock.

"Theo," she moans. "I want you to fuck me hard."

She sucks in a sharp breath as I push inside her, the relief so acute I fucking shudder. I keep one hand under her ass, tearing down her dress with the other,palming her breast. I'm rough this time, it's not a gentle caress, but she loves it, moaning loudly, her nipples so hard they could probably cut me open. I grind my cock into her tight pussy, sliding in deeper and deeper each time, and fuck, she's so wet. Her legs squeeze my hips harder, her mouth open as she pants, as she gasps my name, *Theo, Theo, yeah, fuck, oh god don't stop.*

I bring my mouth down over hers, her lips quivering, her breathing strained. I want to come, I want to come just like this, buried inside her in a wild frenzy because I couldn't fucking stand to wait, but it's too quick, too fast, and if I only have another 12 hours to hear this woman screaming my name as she comes, I'm damn well going to take every chance I get.

I stop my movements with a groan, and Amber rocks her hips, whimpering as she slides herself up and down my length.

"Theo, please," she murmurs, and I pull out of her. "What are you doing?"

Breathing heavy, I turn and carry her up the stairs. She clings on to me, her arms wrapped around my neck. In the bedroom, I put her on her feet, and peel the dress off over her head. She backs away as I strip off my own clothes, lying down on her back with her thighs open, and her eyes widen with delight when I lunge forward to plunge my face into her pussy.

"Theo!" Her fingers claw through my hair, and I clasp onto her thighs to roll onto me back with her on top of my face. She lets out another yelp of surprise, attempting to hover, but I won't have that.

"Sit on my fucking face," I growl. I grip her hips and force her down, sucking her clit hungrily into my mouth.

"*Oh!*" She cries out, her hips jerking in a rhythm that I can tell isn't voluntary. "Theo, fuck, *fuck.*" Her moans are strained, covered by sharp, hissing exhalations. Within seconds she's fucking my face for real, sliding her engorged clit against my tongue, her fingertips raking through my hair.

She may get off on knowing I've lost control, but hearing and feeling and touching her loss of control, her desire and her desperation, is fucking glorious.

I stroke my cock while I pull her clit between my lips, raking gently with my teeth, the sounds she's making sending me even more feral with need.

I'm not going to fucking last. I'm going to explode while she's on my face. The hour in the car, her confession to me about wanting to be used, her delicate fingers stroking my cock, all of it combines into a fiery storm that sears my fucking groin. I groan into her cunt, so wet and dripping, soaking my face.

Her breaths come in short gasps, her thighs trembling violently either side of my head. She tosses her head back, arching her spine with a loud whimper.

"Theo, *fuck*." Her curse is lost in a long moan, and the heat and pressure in my groin is too much.

As Amber screams my name on top of me, I stroke my dick and unleash my own orgasm, painting my stomach in hot jets of cum. My hips jerk as I moan into her, into that sweet pulsating cunt.

Amber runs her fingers gently through my hair, then manoeuvres her shaky legs to climb off me. She slumps to the bed, draping an arm over her face as her chest pounds.

"H-holy shit," she gasps, and swallows hard, more heavy breaths stuttering from between her lips. With a moan, she raises herself to her elbows, and looks over at me. "I thought I was going to pass out."

"Me too," I say with a laugh, grimacing as the cum on my stomach quickly cools.

"Shit, was I too heavy?" Her eyes are wide with alarm.

I run a hand over my face as I laugh, and shake my head. "Honey, you've got to be kidding. *No.*" I arch my neck to raise my head from the bed, taking in her wild hair and her flushed face. "It was that good."

Her mouth curls into a smile. "You really do love eating pussy, don't you?"

"When it's as sweet as yours, yes." I drop my head back to the bed and gaze at the ceiling. "It's fucking incredible."

She shuffles across the bed to lie right next to me, and gently strokes my thigh with the back of her hand. "It's a waste, you know."

"What is?"

"You. Being single. You could be making some woman very happy."

See? It was a game.

I don't say anything, just lie there stroking her legs, staring at the ceiling until my eyes get heavy. I remember the cold mess on my stomach, and wipe it away with a tissue before getting to my feet and cleaning myself properly in the bathroom.

"Do you want a shower?" I call out, but there's no answer.

When I stick my head out the door, Amber is curled up in the bed, the comforter pulled around her shoulders, and she's asleep. I gaze at her for a few minutes, knowing this is the last night I'll see her here like this. After tonight, she'll go back to being my daughter's best friend, and I ask myself over and over how the fuck I'm going to just act like nothing happened.

I climb into the bed, and tuck her into my arms. She sighs in her sleep, nuzzling into me, and within minutes, my eyes close, and I'm asleep too.

———

It's still dark. The wind that picked up earlier in the night is now howling outside the windows.

I blink a few times, my eyes adjusting to the darkness. The only light comes from the full moon flooding through the window, occasionally obscured by fast-moving clouds.

Amber's warm body is still nestled against me, and she's sleeping soundly.

I turn into her with a sigh, nuzzling the crook of her neck to breathe her in. She doesn't stir, just sighs out a soft breath. Her tits are pressed against me, and I run a hand down her side, over her round ass, and instantly I'm hard.

And a thought echoes through my brain. Something she said she wanted to try.

I hesitate, because I've never done this before. Sure, she said she wanted it. But that was the game. We hadn't discussed it again.

In the car this evening she'd said again she wanted to be used. Maybe she meant it then too. Even if it was the game, she wanted to keep playing.

And she's mine til tomorrow.

I gently roll her onto her back, and reach over to the nightstand to retrieve the bottle of lube. Kneeling between her thighs, I coat my cock until I'm slippery, then lift her legs so they're hooked around my elbows. Her brow crinkles, but she keeps sleeping.

This is a rush, a thrill, and it somehow feels even more forbidden, more *wrong*, than anything else I've done to her this weekend. I look down as I guide myself inside her, and she's so impossibly warm and tight, even though her body is relaxed.

I'm halfway inside her when her legs tense slightly. I

stop for a moment, exhaling through gritted teeth at the sensation of having her pussy squeeze me like this. Then I keep going, sinking down, down, and with a sharp groan, I'm inside her, all the way. Panting, I lean over her, looking down at her sleeping face.

"You're so fucking beautiful," I murmur, pulling out so I can slide back inside her, a little deeper this time. I let out a shaky breath, pushing her thighs wider with my arms. "So perfect for me, aren't you, honey?"

Her brow pinches together as I roll in and out of her, but she still doesn't wake, not completely. And because I'm an animal, and this is my last time doing this to her, I pull out completely, just so I can look down to watch her take me again, that slick pussy swallowing me down and clenching me so hard my head spins.

The haze takes over as I fuck her harder, and she's hot and perfect and wonderful. Her legs tense around my arms, and there's a soft gasp. Her head tosses on the bed, lost in that wild tangle of hair, and with a loud moan, her back arches off the bed.

"*Yeah,*" she murmurs, and reaches up to hook her fingers around my neck. "Fuck, harder. Oh my god."

"You said you wanted to wake up with me inside you," I say, slamming my hips against her. "Is this what you imagined?"

She nods, biting her lip, those full tits heaving as she breathes. "Mhmm. Oh god." Her back arches, and I slow my movements.

"Stay with me, honey," I command softly, and her gaze moves back to my face. "I want you to stay right here with me." I reward her with a hard thrust, and her mouth falls open in a cry. "Is this how you want it?"

"Yes," she gasps. "Theo, please... Oh god, harder."

I can see she wants to arch away from me, her body caught in the same haze of euphoria that's taken over mine. But she doesn't move, her body quivering as she stays there with me, both getting hotter and starting to sweat, cries lost in the roaring of the wind outside in the night.

She lets out a loud *Oh!*, her wide eyes fixed on mine, her lips trembling. Her fingers dig into my shoulders, and her hips rock in rhythm with my thrusts, taking me down deeper and deeper every time.

The heat at the base of my spine starts to twist, and Amber's rocking motions send her clit grinding into me with every stroke. The carnal sounds bursting from her lips tell me she's getting closer, and closer, but so am I, so close that I know I'll need to pull out soon, or...

"*Fuck,*" I grit out. "Oh fuck, honey, I have to-"

"*No,*" she cries, her nails clawing at my back. "Oh fuck, Theo, don't stop, please, don't."

I grit my teeth, trying to hold back, but my body fucking ignores me. I'm on autopilot like some sex-crazed fucking robot, punching my cock into her deeper and deeper as my balls draw up tight and hot clawing fingers gash up my spine to match the desperate clawing of Amber's fingers on my skin.

"Amber," I gasp helplessly, stupidly, as though I don't know what's going to happen, as though this hasn't been what I've been dreaming about since this pretty pink pussy was bared to me in my office two days ago. "Honey, I'm going to come." I say it like it'll make a difference. I know it won't.

We don't want to stop.

And we don't.

Amber goes quiet, just for a second, sucking in a breath as her fingertips dig into my skin, and then, like the trip of an electric current, she convulses around me. The violent pulsation of her pussy around my naked cock has me roaring, and I instantly tumble down after her. It feels like I'll never stop coming, my cock pumping her quivering pussy full. It goes on and on, until I drop her legs from my arms, and she reaches up to pull me down to her, kissing me feverishly with her arms wrapped around my neck.

Buried inside her, I kiss her for an eternity, and the wind keeps howling outside. I want to say I shouldn't have done that. I want to say I'm sorry. But I'm not. I'm fucking not. If this is the last time I get to fuck this woman, then I want it to be like this. If that makes me a depraved fuck, then so be it. But knowing I've been inside her gives a sense of satisfaction as though she is mine, and like she'll never be anyone else's, not like this.

"If you were twenty years younger, right?" She breathes against my mouth, and lets out a sad little laugh. "We'd be perfect for each other, right? That's what you said?"

"Yes, honey." I thread my fingers through her hair, my tongue stroking against hers, fucking drunk on kissing her mouth and not knowing how I'm ever supposed to stop. "I'd never let you go. You'd be mine. I'd make sure of it."

"Theo," she whimpers, and wraps her legs around my waist, enveloping me completely. "I-I wish..."

And I know what she's going to say, because I want to say the same thing. I want to say fuck it to everything I know is wrong, everything I know I'm greedy and selfish for wanting.

But I don't.

The sky begins to lighten, the morning finding us still kissing, still feverish and wanting and holding on to every last second as they slip away from us. When I slide back inside her, and fuck her til she's screaming, til she wrings every last drop of my release from my cock, I know I have to let her go.

It was a beautiful dream. A game. A fantasy.

It's over now. That's what we promised ourselves. That's the way it has to be.

8

MONDAY MORNING

I watch as Amber gathers the last of her things from the bedroom, tucking them into her duffel bag. She dresses in a pair of jeans and a light blue sweater, closing the bag with a sigh.

"I think that's all of it," she says, flopping down on the bed beside me. "I guess if you find anything else, you can just..." She shrugs, looking down at her hands. "You can put it in Laurie's room, and she'll find it soon enough."

"Yeah." I don't know what else to say that won't hurt us both, so I just reach out and take her hand.

Amber curls her fingers around mine and sighs.

"You meant it though, right?" Her eyes lift to mine. "If I wasn't me, and you weren't you, and we were the same age..." She trails off, and the question hangs heavy in the air between us.

"I meant it. Really." I stroke her hand. "Maybe in another life. Our next lives, huh?" I raise a hand to her cheek, and give her a soft smile. "I'll be looking out for you."

"I'll make sure I'm born a little sooner next time," she

says with a sad laugh, her face falling. She throws herself at me, wrapping her arms around me, and I bury my face in the crook of her neck. "I'm going to miss this."

"Me, too, honey." I give her a last squeeze, and she pulls back from me slowly. "But it'll be alright. You're going to go out there, and have the whole world at your feet." I sweep her hair back over her shoulder. "You're going to build bridges over the most impossible canyons, go places everyone said you couldn't go. It's all right there, ahead of you. And it's going to be amazing."

She opens her mouth to speak, but her phone buzzes. She exhales heavily, and grabs it from the night stand. Her eyes move over the screen, and then her thumb swipes out a message.

"My parents are on their way back, they'll be home in a couple hours." She lifts her eyes back to my face. "I guess I should go and make it look like I was home all weekend."

"I guess so."

"I'll, uh, see Laurie when she gets back." Amber moves her hand to my arm, but pulls back before her fingers can do more than just brush my skin, and gets to her feet. "I should go."

"Yeah." I should say something more, right? Not just make it sound like I want her to go. I drag my feet to follow her down to the door, surprised when she heads for the garage, then remembering her little stunt on Saturday morning when she no doubt slipped out the side door.

Of course, she can't be seen this time either, leaving my house with a packed bag like she just spent the weekend.

My heart sinks. I want to tell her to stay. I want to ask her to stay forever, and never leave, and whatever anyone thinks be damned.

But I'm too old. I can't tie down a woman this young to a man my age.

She hesitates at the door, turning back to look up at me.

"Thank you," she says quietly.

"You don't have to thank me."

"Yes, I do." She reaches up and strokes my cheek. "You made me feel like I've never felt before, with anyone. And I..." She sighs, her eyes dropping from mine. "I'll never forget it."

"Me neither."

She smiles, still not looking at me. Without another word, she slips through the door and out into the cold Fall morning.

Just like that, she's gone.

I stare at the door for a long time. I don't know what I'm expecting. Maybe I think she'll come running back, like the stupid old fool I am. Everything feels heavy.

Heavy and sad.

The next few hours are spent floating through the day like a lost ghost. Laurie sends me fourteen snaps on her way back from Connecticut, my phone pinging wildly as I change the sheets on my bed. Once the laundry is on and washing, I head to the gym.

I keep my eyes forward, determinedly forward, as I drive past Amber's house. I try to ignore her little blue Golf in the drive.

It's quiet, being a Monday morning, and I work out until my muscles are screaming at me and my body is drenched in sweat. Even the gym manager, Corey, tells me to take it easy when he can see me pushing myself. It's better than thinking about Amber though. This pain I can soothe with a bath and some tiger balm.

God I am a fucking fool, moping like a heartbroken teenager.

I get home, taking the alternative route through the neighbourhood so I don't pass her house again, and head for the shower, feeling the tiniest bit better once I'm clean. Wandering the kitchen and realizing I hate all the food I have in my house, I decide to just fuck it all and order a pizza.

Crippling depression and carb-loading - the day is going great.

I pick up my phone, and there's a couple of pictures from Martin, from his son's baseball game. I don't know why, but I hit the green phone icon, and call Martin's number.

"Hello there little brother," he says in a low voice. "Your busy weekend over?"

I laugh awkwardly. "Yeah, yeah, all over."

"And? When do we meet her?"

I rub the back of my neck as the thought of my family actually meeting Amber makes me break out in sweat. "Oh, no, it's... It's not like that. It was just a casual thing."

"Too much information, Theo." Martin's tone is teasing, and he sniggers quietly. "Not that I'm not happy for you, of course."

"Haha." I roll my eyes, and run my fingertips along the wooden countertop. "Can I ask you something?"

"It'd be kinda weird if I just said no, I guess."

"Did you... I mean, when you were younger, before you were married, did you..." I take a deep breath, wondering how to formulate this question without it sounding really weird. "Did you sleep with a lot of people? I mean, that you weren't in a relationship with?"

Martin chokes out a laugh. "What?"

"I mean... Fuck. What am I trying to say?" I press my thumb and fingers against my closed eyes and growl out a breath. "Did you ever have problems with casual sex? Like, it made you feel gross? You hated one night stands? You only had sex with girlfriends?"

"Oh, you're asking if I'm demisexual?"

My hand drops from my face. "What?"

"Theo, I'm surprised at you." Martin tuts down the phone. "A college professor, with a college aged daughter, who doesn't know about various sexual preferences?"

"You may be my older brother but we both know I could kick your ass."

Martin laughs out loud. "Yeah, yeah, Mr Universe, we know. To answer your question, no, I'm not demisexual. I mean, I wasn't like some manwhore, but I did get around a little at college. I thought you did, too."

I swallow hard. "I did, a little. But, I always found it hard to separate sex and emotions. I found it hard to... have those feelings for someone I didn't know." I squint at the window, where rain has started pattering against the pane again. "Hold up, who explained all this to you?"

"Riley," Martin replies. "She's doing this gender studies class and found out all sorts of things about herself, and then she bombarded us all with these tests so we'd find out where we sat on the scale."

"Your daughter has as inquisitive a mind as you do, I see." I laugh to myself, shaking my head. "Let me guess, she wants to be a sex therapist now."

"How did you know?" Martin chuckles. "Seriously though, I think for us men it's harder to admit something like that to ourselves. First off, we never talked about it growing up. Second, well, we're meant to be sex-crazed and up for it no matter what, no matter when, no matter who, right?"

If only you knew. My cheeks burn with shame.

"I...I guess."

"Does she know?"

I choke a little and clear my throat with a cough. "Wh-who? Know what?"

"Your lady friend," Martin says with a drawl. "Because the way you just said that it was just casual, and now you're talking like this, maybe you should tell her that it meant more to you?"

"No, I can't." I sigh heavily. "She's... Not in a position to be in a relationship."

"Oh, Theo." Martin's voice is instantly strained with concern. "She's not married, is she?"

"No! No, nothing like that, oh my god!" I sputter, trying to come up with some good reason other than admitting the woman I just fucked all weekend til she crawled into my heart and brain was less than half my age and just happened to be my daughter's best friend. "She's just... She's on her way to having an amazing new job, not near here. And I didn't want to hold her back. She made it clear she just wanted... some fun."

"Ah." Martin sighs. "I'm sorry, Theo."

"No, it's fine. I'll be fine. Carb overload, some whiskey, and I'll have forgotten about her before I know it."

"Sure." Martin doesn't sound sure at all, and I know I damn well don't. "Hey, uh, why don't I come down to see you in a couple weeks? Jasper would love to spend some time with his uncle."

"Sure, that'd be great, I'd like that."

"Good."

We both pause awkwardly, not knowing what else to say, and I think if I keep talking the truth will spill out of me and that'll be bad.

"Hey, look, I better go," I say quickly just as Martin begins to speak. "I've got some stuff to do before Laurie gets home."

"Sure, of course. Tell her I said hi."

"Will do!"

I swipe away the call like the phone is on fire and about to reveal all my secrets.

It's fine. I'll be fine.

I lean heavily on the countertop, my phone pinging to let me know the driver is on their way with my pizza. I open the app, the words swimming in front of me, and I look around on the counter for my glasses. They're not there.

They must be on my desk.

I head into the office, and sure enough, there they are. I round the desk, and step on something soft with my bare foot. I look down, and my heart lurches when I see it's a pair of Amber's lacy panties. My face is on fire, and I feverishly pace the house for any more traces of her, because how in the fuck would I ever explain that to my daughter. Sure, those panties could belong to anyone, it's not like they have a big bold sign printed on them saying, *Property of the 20 year old woman your father fucked all over the house while you were away for the weekend. Oh, and she's also your best friend.*

At the end of my search, I'm left with two pairs of Amber's panties. The pair from the office, and the pair that I made her take off at the restaurant. They were still tucked into my pocket. I stare at them before stuffing them into my night stand, to be dealt with later. I can't very well leave those lying in Laurie's room to be returned later.

I take a deep, steadying breath, and scold myself for being so damned anxious.

It was what it was. It's over now. No one has to know. Put it behind you, old man.

By the time Laurie returns that night, I've almost convinced myself that I can.

9

19 MONTHS LATER

THE LATE SPRING breeze wafting in through the window is warm and heady with the promise of a hot Summer. The golden afternoon sun washes across the yard, and everything is dreamy and hazy - the perfect weather for a celebration.

I check my pockets for my phone, keys and wallet, then look around on the kitchen counter for my glasses and sunglasses.

"Laurie!" I call for what feels like the tenth time. "We got places to be, peanut!"

"I'm almost done!" Comes the distant reply.

"You said that half an hour ago!" I chuckle to myself, shaking my head. I check my phone to find a message from Mella, saying she's at the house we've hired in the next town over for the graduation party. I type out a quick reply, telling her we'll be on our way once our daughter stops preening.

A few seconds later, Laurie's rushed footsteps patter down the stairs, and she bursts into the kitchen. She's wearing a white Grecian style one-shoulder dress, her blonde hair hanging in glossy curls around her shoulders. Big, sparkly earrings set with orange stones dangle from her ears. She tugs nervously at the hemline of her dress as her big blue eyes meet mine.

"Do I look... OK?" She asks uncertainly.

I puff out a heavy breath, and shake my head as it hits me full force that my daughter is a woman, a grown woman with a college degree and a career waiting on her. She's about to make her own way in the world, a world far, far away from me.

"No, peanut, you do not look OK." I smile when her eyebrows almost disappear into her shiny blonde bangs. "You look absolutely radiant. The most beautiful girl in the world."

Her face melts into a smile, and she wraps me in a hug. "Thanks, daddy."

"Oh, peanut." I kiss the top of her head. "When did you go on and grow up, huh?"

"It sort of happened a while ago."

"Well, it's extremely rude if you ask me. It went by way too fast." I give her shoulders a squeeze as she giggles. "Come on now, time to go celebrate. They're all waiting for you."

Laurie furiously taps at her phone as we drive through the neighbourhood and down the back road out of town.

"Everyone is so excited," she says, bouncing in her seat. "I still can't believe you all put this huge party on for us."

"All you college graduates deserve it. You worked so damn hard this past year." I look over at her, and she gives me a smile. "Besides, you need to get in as much sunshine as you can before you move to Seattle."

"*Ha, ha,*" she drawls. "I happen to like the rain."

I grunt out a laugh. "Good, you won't have much choice soon."

"Dad, stop it," she scolds, but her voice is light. Her phone pings again, and she snatches it up from the dash. "Oh, Amber's there! She just arrived. God, I missed her *so* much, I feel like I haven't seen her in forever!"

Great. I clear my throat, trying to clear the dry lump that forms there immediately at the mention of Amber's name. I cover it all with a cough, trying not to make my nerves so obvious to my daughter, who continues to tap away at her phone.

"Didn't you all just go to Mexico in, what, May?" I'm trying desperately to sound jovial, not like my heart is threatening to thump right out of my chest.

"It's not the same though. Not when you're around all those people and have fiances in tow." Laurie shrugs with a little sigh. "But I guess it's how it's going to be now, with me all the way over on the west coast. Everything's changing."

I'm ashamed of myself that I'm more caught up on the word *fiancé* than I am in comforting my daughter about the huge life changes ahead of her. But my stomach does that drop, the same drop it did back at Christmas when Laurie squealed into her phone the night before Christmas Eve. *Amber got engaged*, she'd cried, and shoved the phone into my face so I could admire Amber's beautiful new engagement ring. Amber and I had made almost the exact same face as we'd stared at each other for the first time since our weekend together the year before.

I mumbled out some congratulations before Laurie had snatched the phone away from me to disappear into her room as she and Amber discussed wedding dress. More cry-screaming when Laurie yelled down the stairs, *I'm going to be maid of honour!*

I'd taken a bottle of whiskey to my room and downed too much of it while watching the Hallmark Holiday marathon. And yes, after too much whiskey and one too many heartfelt confessions of love in front of snow-covered inns in rural Vermont, I'd cried.

Amber was engaged. She had a *fiancé*.

I hadn't intentionally avoided Amber since our weekend together.

OK, that's a lie. Maybe I had, although I still don't want to admit that to myself.

I had tried to convince myself that it wouldn't be a problem. That I could totally handle seeing her again, and be nothing but friendly with her, just like I had been before.

Then the first time she had come to my house with Laurie, I'd heard her voice in the downstairs hall and practically ran back to my room, hiding like a fool and feigning sleep when Laurie knocked on the door.

The demands of college meant that, as time had gone on, those visits home became less frequent, and when Laurie and Amber were at home at the same time, they spent a lot of time at Mella's. Whether that was Amber's idea, and whether she, too, was actively avoiding me, I don't know. Either way, when they were at my house, I'd lock the door to my office and hide, insisting I was busy working.

Our promise that nothing would change between us had been broken, and I was sure I was the one who'd broken it, because Amber had moved on. In spectacular fashion too. I'd heard about the new boyfriend one evening when Laurie and I were having dinner, and she assured me this one was *serious*. I focused too much on the *this one*, and my jealous ass wondered how many there had been since me.

Which made me a complete fool, since I'd dated women too. Only a few. And I'd never been able to settle down or commit to any of them. I'd always found a reason to let them go.

But seven months later, Amber was engaged.

I guess this one really was serious.

I shift in my seat as Laurie cackles at the messages from friends that keep pouring in, her phone buzzing almost constantly. I tell myself to get it together. This is Laurie's night, celebrating her graduation. Whatever stupid, sentimental, old man feelings I have, they're not important. And while seeing Amber with her fiancé wouldn't be easy, it was what it was. I'd get over it. This is what I'd wanted for her, right?

Just get over yourself, Rembrook. Be fucking happy for her.

The parking lot of the old country house is full when we pull up, and I recognise a few of the cars. My parents are here, as well as Martin and his family. Amber's parents are parked right next to Mella's car, and a man with reddish hair like Amber's is retrieving two pre-school aged kids from an SUV while a pretty brunette stands beside him with an indulgent smile on her face as the kids fuss.

"That's Amber's oldest brother!" Laurie exclaims, and waves to the man and his partner as we pass. They wave back with big smiles, and the kid pauses their fussing to wave back. "Have you met Kieran?"

"No, he'd already moved out when I bought the house."

"He's really sweet." Laurie giggles as she smoothes her dress over her legs. "He gave Ryan hell when he and Amber first started dating, oh my god." She giggles, and my face flushes as I try to imagine the hell Kieran would give me if he knew what I'd done with his little sister.

Shut the fuck up and stop thinking about that.

I park my car, and get out to help Laurie pick her way across the dirty parking lot. My sister Felicity pulls up as we reach the front door, and Laurie jumps up and down waving. My sister's son, Jackson, gets out of the car and barrels towards us, scooping Laurie up in his arms,

"We did it, cuz!" He says as Laurie shrieks. He puts Laurie down and ignores my outstretched hand, grabbing me in a bear hug.

I laugh and pat my nephew's back, and I swear this kid has to be 6'7 at least. "You sure did, Jacks! Congratulations."

"Head of his class, did I tell you?" My sister calls, her face glowing with pride.

"You told me, at least 60 times." I finally extract myself from my nephew's hug, and pat his shoulder. "I'm proud of you, Jacks."

"Thanks, Theo."

"Come *on!*" Laurie tugs on Jackson's sleeve, and they both run into the house as Felicity takes my arm and plants a kiss on my cheek.

"How many times have you cried?" She asks me, and I laugh.

"Only about seventeen. Since 9am."

Felicity laughs and shakes her head. "It's not easy when you only have one, is it?" She leans against my shoulder with a sigh as we walk into the house, following the sound of music and excited chatter. "One minute, they're a tiny baby in your arms, the next, they're braving this big world on their own while all we can do is watch."

"What did mom always say? The days are long-"

"But the years are short," Felicity finishes for me, and her voice wobbles. "They sure are."

I pat her hand as we approach the open double doors at the back of the house, which lead out to the enormous yard. The trees are hung with fairy lights that glitter amongst the lush foliage, music wafts through the air, and the entire scene is bathed in the hazy light of early evening. The air is warm and scented with honeysuckle, and people turn to wave as they spot us.

Laurie is laughing and talking at volume with her cousins and her friends, and Mella is talking to my parents, her new husband at her side.

I tell myself my eyes aren't scanning the yard for Amber, that I'm just looking for more of my family. I know I damn well shouldn't be looking for her. I'm steeling myself for the gut punch when I finally see her on the arm of her fiance, probably some young tech bro, some ridiculously handsome young man with perfect white teeth and smooth hair that doesn't have a single strand of gray. Probably tanned and dressed in fucking Ralph Lauren.

Easy, man. Calm down.

I exhale through gritted teeth, and Felicity looks up at me with raised eyebrows.

"Something wrong?"

I quickly shake my head, forcing a smile and looking out over the yard.

And there she is.

Amber's standing by the old barn, a glass of champagne in her delicate fingers, talking to a young man who has his back to me. She's smiling up at him, her skin glowing against the electric blue of her dress. Her hair is so long now, hanging down almost to her ass in a curly, swept-back low ponytail. The dress is short and shows off her long legs, which look even longer in the heels she's wearing.

She raises the glass to her lips, taking a sip as she smiles and nods, her gaze wandering from the man's face - and straight to mine.

My heart stops.

The smile fades from her lips, and we're probably making this really fucking obvious, just staring at each other across the yard. She's standing next to the man I assume is her fiancé, and she's staring right at another man.

"Theo?" My sister's voice jolts me back to reality, and I remember where I am and what I'm meant to be doing.

I clear my throat and look down at my sister with a smile. "Sorry, zoned out for a second. There's so many people here."

I cast another glance over at Amber, who's resumed her conversation with the man, but her eyes flash in my direction. I force myself to look away, and go to greet my family and Mella.

I make pleasant small talk, and someone presses a drink into my hand, which I drink without even tasting it or thinking about what it is. I try not to look for Amber, because that would be creepy, but I can't help but somehow be aware of where she is, warm like the sun as she moves around the party.

The man I assumed was her fiancé turns out to be the brother of one of the other boys here, and I can't help but wonder where her fiancé is. He should be at this party. It's an important night for Amber. The fact he's not in attendance makes me irrationally angry.

After making more small talk and drinking more drinks I don't even pay attention to, my brain starts to feel fuzzy.

I'm almost worn out from being so hyper-aware of where Amber is, and I excuse myself to go to the bathroom to try and take a breath and get a handle on myself. This isn't helpful, or healthy.

The music fades as I move through the house, past the kitchen where the caterers are busily preparing more food.I turn a corner, into a room furnished with just an artfully beige bookshelf, and a desk under the window. I stand in the middle of the room and look out at the fading light, and take a deep breath.

Calm down, man. You're putting way too much thought into this. It was one weekend, almost two years ago. The girl's moved on. You'll barely see her anymore after tonight. Just let it go.

"Theo?"

The sweet voice makes my heart propel through my body like a tornado.

I spin around, and Amber's standing there in the door-way, her hand with pretty white-tipped nails against the door frame. Her lips lift into a small, uncertain smile.

"Hi," she says softly.

"Hi." All I can say is that one stupid word.

Amber steps into the room, fidgeting with her hands. "You look really nice."

"I, uh, thanks, I mean... You do... too. Look gorgeous. I mean."

She giggles, her cheeks flushing pink. "Thank you." She takes another step closer. "It's really good to see you."

"You, too." I want to apologise for not seeing her, for not talking to her, for not doing anything I should have done in the past... How long has it been? I had a counter going. 500 days? More? I don't know. I should know. But I don't do that. "I guess congratulations are in order. I heard you made Valedictorian."

She tucks a strand of hair behind her ear, and shrugs. "Yeah. I did. It was, ummm... I guess I really found my calling."

"I told you, Amber Pope, future bridge builder." I take a deep breath and look at the ground. "I guess it won't be Amber Pope for much longer though, huh?" I look back up at her, unprepared for the pain in her face. "I mean... Shit. Sorry, I didn't mean that to sound-"

"We broke up."

I suck in a breath, my brows drawing down into a frown. "I... What?"

"My fiancé, and I. We... We broke up. A couple of months ago." Amber lets out a short, cynical laugh. "I'm surprised Laurie didn't tell you. But then why would she? It's not like we're anything to each other, right?"

"Honey..." I want to punch myself in the face for even calling her that, and I take a step towards her. "Amber, what happened?"

She looks out the window with a shrug. "I realised I was play-acting. Pretending. Pretending to be happy with some-thing that I wasn't really happy with, because I told myself I should be." Her eyes move back to me, and they're shin-ing, like she's about to cry. "We should have been perfect together. He was sweet, handsome, really nice. His folks liked me. And when he asked me to marry him it felt like it was the right thing to do."

"I'm... I'm so sorry."

She gives me a pained smile. "I was determined, you know? After we... I was determined to go out and use that confidence to find what I thought I was looking for." She reaches out a tentative hand to draw her fingertips along my jaw, and her touch is electric, and warm. "I tried. I really did. Because I told myself that what we had was just one weekend. It's crazy to hold on to that, right? Something we said wouldn't mean anything."

But it did mean something. I don't think it's the right time to say that to her, not when it won't help and it sure as fuck won't stop the hurt that's lingering in her eyes. She draws closer to me, and I can smell her perfume, fresh and sweet like those apple orchards she told me about.

"Honey..." I lift a hand to her face, and a single tear slips down her cheek. "I..."

"*Am*-ber!" The insistent call is accompanied by staccato taps of stilettos on the hardwood floor.

Amber and I spring apart, just in time, as Laurie stalks past the door, doubling back when she spots us.

"There you are!" She shimmies in, holding out her hands to Amber with a wide grin. "Come on, babe, it's time for toasts!"

"Yeah, oh, OK." Amber clears her throat, and Laurie frowns.

"Babe?" She looks at me with alarm, then back at Amber. "Amber, are you alright? Are you crying?"

"No, no, I'm fine, I mean, um yeah, just emotional." Amber throws me a quick, forced smile. "Just a lot going on. I told your dad about, um, my new job."

"Yes, she did." I smile at my daughter who still looks concerned and now a little confused. "Big things are happening."

"Ohhhh." Laurie smiles and shrugs, slipping an arm around Amber's shoulders. "Are you crying because it's Boston?"

"Boston?" I ask. "You hate Boston."

STUPID. MOTHER. FUCKER.

Amber looks at me with alarm, and Laurie is even more confused.

"What?" Laurie asks with a laugh. "How do you know she hates Boston?"

"We should go, they're waiting for us." Amber grabs Laurie's hand and drags her out of the room.

"Come on, dad!" Laurie calls after her.

I stare at the door like an asshole for a minute before forcing myself out into the yard. The fairy lights illuminate the garden, the sky turning brilliant shades of orange and pink as the sun sets. Martin hands me a drink and asks me something, and I just nod stupidly. I don't even know what he asked me.

There are speeches, Amber's father saying how proud he is of his daughter, and Amber smiles sweetly at him. My stupid haze is broken for a few minutes when Mella hauls me up with her and insists we both give a speech for Laurie. We tell her how proud we are, how bright her future is, and how glad we are that we get to be her parents. Laurie starts to cry into my mother's shoulder, and my family mills around her and comforts her. Once our speech is done, Laurie runs into our arms and hugs us both. Mella and I smile at each other, a little awkwardly at first, but we focus on our daughter, still weeping between us, and relax.

Drinks continue to flow as the other parents get up and give their speeches, everyone cheering on the new gradu-ates. The mood is light, we're all having a good time, and yet I can't help it that my eyes keep drifting in Amber's direction. Music starts to boom over the speakers, the grad-uates and their siblings breaking into a dance as they sing along to a song I recognize but don't know the words to.

Another drink in my hand, I try to avoid the hundreds of questions my mother throws at me about the last woman I was dating. Martin thankfully intervenes, talking about his latest medical conference in Paris.

Across the garden, Amber disappears down the side of the barn. The way she glances around before she moves out of sight, checking that she's alone and nobody is watching, has butterflies swooping through my stomach. Excusing myself from my family, I try to look as casual as possible, ambling towards the barn.

I pause at the corner, looking over the party, checking no one's eyes are turned this way right now. Because I'm a fucking criminal and know what I'm about to do is so, so wrong. Sure everyone is distracted, I turn and hurry down the side of the barn, rounding the corner, and stop short.

Amber is leaning against the wall, her hands tucked behind her, her eyes fixed on me, knowing exactly I was coming to follow her. Even in the semi-darkness, the desire in her face is more than obvious.

"You found me," she murmurs.

I should say something. We should talk. We should *really* talk.

But like the fool that I am, I don't say anything, because being this close to her, being alone with her again after all this time, sets my blood roaring.

I rush at her, pinning her against the wall and taking her face in my hands as my mouth comes down to meet hers. She kisses me back eagerly, not a hint of hesitation as her trembling fingers curl around the back of my neck.

"We shouldn't be doing this," I breathe against her mouth, and she nibbles at my lips. "I... I should be better than this."

"You think I don't want this?" She pulls me closer, pressing her body wrapped in that fucking sexy blue dress against me. "You think I haven't dreamed of you losing control the minute you saw me again?"

My mouth comes down on hers again, although I know

damn well at any moment someone could round that corner and the whole game would be up. Here, at my daughter's fucking graduation party, I'm in the arms of her best friend like a dirty old man.

"Take me home," Amber murmurs, gazing up at me. "I want you to take me home, and take me to bed. I missed you so much."

I let her go with a heavy breath, hands braced against the wall either side of her. "Amber, we need to talk."

"I don't want to talk," she says, her mouth hovering close to mine. "No talking now. I just need you to fuck me."

My hands curl into fists as I try to maintain my self-control. "Amber, we can't do this."

"How many times did you watch our videos?" Her lips curl into a smile against mine as I suck in a breath. "How many times do you think I watched them?" Her hands drop to my belt. "Do you know how many nights I lay in my bed, watching those videos and making myself come, dreaming of you?"

"*Amber.*" I put a shaking hand to her cheek, and she nips at me, taking my lower lip between her teeth. I groan at the sensation and push her back against the wall. "Honey, we... we can't."

"But you want to." Her hands run down my back, to my ass, and she grinds herself against me. "Do you know how wet I am right now, thinking about you?"

I'm a good man. I'm better than this. I am fucking better than this.

Except I'm not.

Because I lean into her, kissing her ferociously, cupping her breast in my hand, earning me a sweet little whimper. I want nothing more than to put a hand between her legs and see just how wet she is for me. She opens her legs to grind herself against my thigh, and gasps into my mouth. "Theo," she murmurs, in that tone I've missed so much, the voice that's been the star of my dreams every single fucking night. "*Theo*."

The moment is shattered when a firework goes off above our heads. I jump away from her, and in the showering light of the falling embers, Amber's lips are full and parted, her hair dishevelled, her dress riding up her thighs. She's beautiful, and she wants me. I should see that. I should see her. But all I can see as I look at this woman who just begged me to take her home, are all the people out there, the people who love us, finding out what I've done to her.

Amber gives me a slow smile, and reaches for me.

"Come back here," she says, and bites her lip.

"I can't." I want to fucking die at the look she gives me.

She lowers her hands, frowning, shaking her head. "I-I don't understand-"

"Honey, we can't do this. I'm... I'm sorry. But..." I run my hands through my hair with a growl. "We just can't do this."

"You don't want me?" She asks in a shaky voice, and I want to say yes, I do want her.

I want to say that I want her more than air because the past two years have been fucking torture. Because I never stopped thinking about her. Because I watched those videos every single fucking day, even the ones I knew I should erase, where she's moaning my name and I'm roaring hers as I come. That I lay awake at night aching for her warmth against my chest. That waking up every morning alone is miserable. That I fucking *cried* when she got engaged. That my heart belongs to her because I'm a fool who fell for her in the space of 72 hours.

But I know that if I don't finish this now, it'll never be done, not for her. I'll always be the good man, the one who got away, the one who she dreams about. No man will ever measure up, not if I don't destroy that image she has in her head. I can't hold on to her. She can't keep me.

It needs to stop. So I end it, the only way I know how.

"No, I don't."

Amber gasps, her eyes dropping from mine. Her hand flies to her mouth, and I hate myself.

"Amber, I'm sorry, but... you're too young. You're a girl. You don't know what you want."

Her eyes flash to mine, filled with pain and tears. "Yes I do. I *do*."

"No you don't." I shake my head. "We had a great weekend together, it was a lot of fun. But it was just sex. Good sex isn't all there is to a relationship, and the fact you think it is shows me you're too immature for this."

"Immature?" She rushes at me and shoves me in the chest. "How can you say that to me?"

"Go back to the party, honey." I seize her wrists, and look down at her sternly. "Go to Boston, and forget about me. Forget about all of it. It didn't mean anything, remember?"

"Fuck you!" She covers her face with her hands, her shoulders shaking as she cries.

Fix this. Fix it now. Fucking say something, you goddamn coward.

But she runs away from me before I can say anything.

Fireworks keep going off above my head, and the people I love, my family, my daughter, cheer and laugh and celebrate.

But I know that somewhere, a woman is crying her eyes out because of me. I ruined her graduation party, I ruined her memories of our time together, and I became just like all the other assholes who hurt her.

Even at my big age, I still managed to act like a little shit, and make her feel used.

You really don't deserve her.

I float through the rest of the night, trying not to notice when Amber's mother comes out of the house, concern on her face as she says something to her husband. He frowns and hands her a set of car keys, and she waves him off with a sad smile.

Amber's mother leaves, and when Laurie asks where Amber is, someone says that she went home because she was sick.

I can't take it anymore, and ask Mella to drive Laurie home.

I leave the party quietly, not wanting to ruin Laurie's fun.

Then I go home, down half a bottle of whiskey, and pass out in my bed, hoping to god I don't dream of tear-filled brown eyes and that sweet voice calling my name.

Of course, I fucking do.

10

THREE WEEKS AFTER THE PARTY

"WELL, that's the last of it," Laurie announces, taping the last box and scrawling *Bedroom - Dads H* on the top in black sharpie. She gets to her feet and gazes around the room that was her teenage bedroom, before her eyes land on me. "I can't believe this is it."

"Me neither." I cross my arms and lean against the door frame. "I mean, if you're really nice I might not rent it out right away. I might even let you come home for Christmas sometimes."

"How generous of you, thank you, father." Laurie grins as she picks up the box, shaking her head when I hold out my hands to take it from her. "I got it, dad."

I follow my extremely capable daughter down to the U-haul she rented to move her life across the country to Seattle.

"You going to be OK driving this thing?" I ask as she slides the box into the back.

"Yeah I'll be fine." She rolls the door down and dusts off her hands. "Mom said she's driven these before too, so I'm pretty confident we'll be all set."

"I wish I could be the one to drive you, peanut."

Laurie waves me off with a smile. "It's fine, dad. Mom's really excited to do this with me. Besides, you're coming to see me before the summer's out, right?"

"I sure am."

Laurie's phone pings, and she pulls it from her pocket. "Aww, poor Amber."

My stomach does a flip. "Everything alright?"

"Yeah, yeah, she's just..." Laurie trails off as she taps out a response. "Having a hard time. I thought it was the break-up with Ryan, but... It seems to be something else."

"Oh, jeez. I wonder what it could be." I hope I sound fucking nonchalant, because I feel anything but. The guilt has been eating me up for the past three weeks, since that awful night at the graduation party.

Laurie sighs. "I think it's the move to Boston."

"Yeah, probably."

Laurie looks at me with raised eyebrows and heads back into the house. "I'm thirsty, let's get a drink before I go."

I follow her into the kitchen, and Laurie gets out two glasses and pours us both a lemonade.

"You know," she says slowly, sliding the glass towards me. "I think Amber wouldn't be so nervous about moving to Boston if she was going with someone."

"Oh, yeah?" I take a sip of the lemonade, and don't meet Laurie's eyes. "Which someone?"

"Dad."

I try to swallow down the lemonade, which is about as easy as swallowing broken glass, and raise my eyes to Laurie's. Her eyebrows are still raised, and she's tapping a finger against the counter.

"You can drop the act, Dad."

My head whirs. Blood roars in my ears. My mouth is dry

even though I just had a drink, and Laurie's eyes bore into me.

"Wh-what act, peanut?" I shake my head, and Laurie puffs out a laugh.

"Dad, come on. It would only be more obvious if you were wearing a t-shirt saying, *I'm in Love with Amber Pope.*"

My stomach turns into a stone and drops through the floor. My throat swells up and I scramble to say something, anything. But I just gawp like a damn fish, staring at my daughter, who sighs and shakes her head.

"Dad-"

"I'm so sorry." I reach across the counter to take Laurie's hand, shame welling up in my chest. "I know you must think I'm disgusting, and a pervert. But you have to know, I never meant for this to happen. I never thought of her that way when you were kids, I swear. I never once-"

"Dad, it's OK." Laurie dips her head to meet my eyes, and smiles. "I promise. I'm not angry. Really, I'm not."

I exhale heavily. "How can you be alright with this? It's... It's wrong."

"Two people loving each other isn't wrong."

"It is when one of them is as old as I am," I scoff. "I never should have done it. She came over, and was so... Pretty, and... I was stupid, and weak. And now... Now I just hurt her." I look up at my daughter's narrowed eyes, and instantly feel ashamed all over again. "How did you even figure it out?"

"I had my suspicions when you suddenly wouldn't be in the same room together anymore." Laurie chuckles when I cover my face with my hands. "But the whole, *You hate Boston* thing just sort of confirmed it."

"Fuck." I drag my hands down my face and meet my

daughter's sympathetic gaze. "It can't happen. It just can't. I can't do that to her."

"Do what, dad? Make her happy? Make her feel loved?" Laurie throws her hands up. "I am really failing to see what the problem is here. The only thing that pisses me off is I can't ask her about all the gory details because, Eww." She wrinkles her nose for a second. "But that's it. There is nothing standing in the way of this."

"Laurie, come on." I get to my feet and stalk along the kitchen counter, raking my hands through my hair and despite feeling intense shame, I'm also so relieved that someone knows, even if that someone is my daughter. "I'm pushing fifty. She's just turned twenty-two. Her whole life is ahead of her. She doesn't want some old man at her side, weighing her down."

"First of all, you're not old," Laurie says, holding up a finger in the air. "Further to that, you are not the average dad. You work out every single day. Your legs are the size of a small child. You're fit, and you're healthy, and I don't think a walker and a bed pan are in your near future."

I can't help but laugh at her words and the indignant look on her face. "Fine. I'm fit and healthy. So what? People die all the time, even when they're fit."

"Fucking *exactly*." Laurie throws her hands up again and groans. "So Amber marries some finance bro and he gets hit by a Maserati on Wall Street the next year, was she never supposed to get married in case that happened?"

"That is not the point," I say, rubbing my temples with a sigh. "Of course anyone can die at any time. But Amber deserves a full life, with the best chance of having a partner at her side for a long time. I might only be able to give her another twenty-five years, what then? You want her to be a widow when she's in her forties?"

Laurie folds her arms over her chest and fixes me with a look that makes me feel very much like the child being taught a life lesson. "Let's flip that around. Say you really only do have twenty-five years left. Twenty-five more Christmases. Twenty-five more summers. Twenty-five more days of going down to the pumpkin patch and picking out your carving pumpkins for Halloween. Who do you want to spend those twenty-five years with?"

I huff out a frustrated breath as I lean on the counter. "It is not that simple. Her family will not approve, her father will kill me, her brothers will probably help and can you even imagine what your mother would say?"

"Umm, hello?" Laurie waves her hand directly in my face. "What about what I think?"

I stutter out a breath, trying to come up with another argument, but feeling more and more defeated in the face of my daughter's determined reason. "What do you think?"

"I happen to think it's just fine." Laurie puffs out a breath and runs her blond braid through her hands. "But you are way too caught up on what everyone else thinks, and not what Amber thinks, or what she wants. Anyone who loves her will accept you both, even if it takes a minute, because she'd be happy. You parentals talked our *whole* lives about our happiness being all that mattered. Was that true or not?"

"Of course it was."

Laurie's eyebrows shoot back up into her bangs. "But?"

"Only if it doesn't hurt you," I say weakly.

"You're not going to hurt Amber." Laurie's expression softens. "I always tell her she deserves the best, because she does. She's my person, you know? And, if it came down to the best men in the world that I know would treat her right, you'd be at the top of that list."

I collapse back into the stool and drop my head into my hands. "Too late. I broke her heart at the graduation party. I was an idiot, and she won't forgive me for what I said."

"Dad, seriously, you need to stop guessing what people are going to say before they say it." Laurie gets to her feet, and puts her arms around me. "We all make mistakes, right? But nothing that can't be fixed."

I hug my daughter, and want to tell her that some things just can't be fixed. Some words cut too deep and can't be taken back. But I don't want to disillusion her, and maybe I really am just a coward who doesn't want to confront all of this. Who's too scared of what this will all do to his reputation, rather than worrying about the woman he loves.

Great partner material I am.

"You should hit the road," I say after a minute, and kiss the top of her head. "Your mom will be waiting for you."

"OK, daddy." She hugs me tighter for a second, and I hug her back. My kiddo. My little girl. Leaving the house for good. "I'll let you know when we stop for the night."

"Do that." I keep my arm around her shoulders as I walk her back out to the U-haul. "And I'll see you in August."

"I can't wait." She climbs into the truck and guns the engine, giving me a wide smile as I close the door for her. "Try not to miss me too much."

"You know I will." I tuck my hands into my pockets as I step back from the truck.

She puts on music, singing at the top of her lungs as she pulls out of the drive, waving madly out of the open window. I can't help but laugh, shaking my head as the thumping music fades away in the distance.

I stand in my driveway for a long time, the hot sun beating down on my shoulders. I look down the street in the direction of Amber's parents' house. I don't even know if she's still there, and I can't very well go over there. *Hello, excuse me Aaron, I'm in love with your daughter and I'd like to see her.*

That's a great way to get my nose broken.

I rub the back of my neck with a sigh, turning to go back into the house. I fucked up. I know I did. I hurt an amazing woman who made me feel more myself than I ever have in my life, all because I'm a fucking coward.

I may not be able to win her back. But I can apologize. That's the least I can do.

The butterflies erupt all over again the second I pick up my phone. The last messages in the conversation with Amber are the damn videos I sent her. What a follow-up this is going to be.

But it has to be done.

> I know I'm probably the last person you want to hear from now, but I wanted to say I'm sorry. I'm sorry for ruining your graduation party. I'm sorry for what I said to you. And most of all I'm sorry for lying to you. Because none of what I said that night was true. You're incredible, and I've thought about you every day since that weekend with you. I know I've messed things up and I don't expect you to forgive me. I don't deserve it. But you're the most amazing woman I ever met. You made me feel like Me for the first time in a long time. And even if you never talk to me again, I want you to know I was wrong. It was all me, my stupidity, my cowardice. It was never you. And even though I know I shouldn't be, I'll never stop being glad that you walked into my house that afternoon. I wish you nothing but happiness, and contentment. And the man who finally doesn't fuck things up with you is going to be luckiest son of a bitch on earth.

I stare at the words for a long time, deleting the word earth and retyping it 8 times, before finally just hitting send. *Get it over with.*

After a few minutes, the little green tick comes up showing that Amber's read my message. I hold my breath for so long my chest becomes tight. Then the three little dots that show she's typing bounce on the screen. Then stop. Then start again. Then stop.

And nothing.

After 10 minutes I give up, and close the message. I meant it. If she never talks to me again, I have to be alright with that. She needed to know it wasn't her, that it never was. She's perfect.

I'm just a stupid old fool who still can't figure all this love shit out.

————

The night is warm, the birds singing in the trees as the last of the orange streaks painting the sky fade away. I finish washing up after my solitary dinner of the leftover pasta Laurie cooked last night, and head out onto the porch.

A soft breeze blows through the trees, and I walk to the steps, gazing up at the stars as they start to twinkle in the blue-grey sky. If it's hot again tomorrow, I might go swimming instead of going to the gym.

A deer wanders along the edge of the forest, two babies staggering along behind her on their too-long, gangly legs. The mother looks up, her ears twitching, and suddenly she dashes off into the forest, her babies following close behind.

I pad down the steps and dig my toes into the grass, which is still holding on to the last warmth of the sun.

A car door slams close by and I turn in the direction of the sound. Keys jangle, and then there's the rhythmic slap of flip-flops on concrete. Someone is running down the side of my house. I move closer, not knowing what to expect, when Amber comes flying around the corner.

She stops short when she sees me, clutching her keys to her chest. Her long hair is loose, and she's wearing denim shorts and a tiny white tank top, a floaty pink shirt draped over the top. Her face is red and ruddy, her eyes shining, like she's been crying.

Alarmed, relieved, fucking ecstatic but not daring to hope, I stumble towards her. "Amber, what are you doing here?"

She inhales sharply, then hurtles across the yard at me. She jumps right into my arms, and I'm ready to catch her. I clutch her to me as she wraps her arms and legs around me, and her lips descend on mine in a feverish rush. I don't even have time to think that this is really happening, because my brain is so flooded with bliss and happiness. She's here, in my yard, in my arms, kissing me, when I thought she'd never speak to me again.

"Fuck you!" She cries suddenly, pulling back from me and slapping me in the chest over and over. "You stupid, stupid asshole!"

"I am, I'm a huge, stupid, idiotic asshole."

"Yes you are." Tears stream down her face as she leans her forehead against mine. "Do you know how long I fucking cried over you?"

"I'm sorry. I'm so, so sorry, honey. I can't even tell you how sorry I am."

She kisses me, sobbing softly. "I was halfway to my grandparents' house when I got your damn message." She pulls back from me with a sad smile and shakes her head. "I drove so fast coming back here, I think I got a speeding ticket."

"Oh, honey, I shouldn't have done that, you could have-"

"Yes, yes you fucking should have. You should have followed me that night, you should have... You should have..." She burrows her face against my neck and starts to sob louder.

"I'm so sorry, Amber." I drop into a kneel with her in my lap, holding her to me. "I was such a fucking idiot. I didn't... I didn't want to tie you down to a man my age. You deserve more, so much more than I can give you."

"Shut up!" She pushes against my chest, her furious,

teary eyes meeting mine. "You don't get to decide what I do and do not deserve. And you sure as hell don't get to push me away over some bullshit about your age."

"I know, honey. I'm sorry. What I said to you at the graduation party... It was so wrong."

"It *wasn't* just sex," she says, her voice strained as more tears start to fall. "I hate that you reduced it to that. It was so much more. I'm not some airhead who can't tell the difference."

"I know, I know."

She grips my face in her hands and tips my head back. "Stop. Talking. Stop saying, *I know, I know,* and just *listen* to me."

I have to suppress a smile because she's so fiery and angry and determined, and all I want to do is kiss her. But I sit silently and let her get it all out.

"I didn't expect to feel the way I do about you, and I know that was probably stupid of me." Her lips tremble, and she licks away tears that have gathered in the corners of her mouth. "I liked you, I really did. But I told myself I was making it into something bigger than it was. After I left I talked myself out of it, you know? That it was nothing, it was dumb, and it was just a crush. That I was dickmatized because it had been the best sex of my life."

I want to ask what the fuck dickmatize means, but I decide that if I interrupt her now she'll probably claw my eyes out and I'll like it, so I keep my mouth shut.

"I tried, Theo." She sniffles, raising her eyebrows. "I did. I tried so *fucking* hard. I went out and dated, I had more mediocre sex, and then... Then I met Ryan." Her voice falters a little on his name. "He was sweet. He was funny, and handsome. So I tried. Because it made sense. Like you're always saying, he was young and could give me all that shit that lies ahead of me. I fell into what I thought my life should be, and I tried so *fucking hard* to be happy in that life." She hiccups out another sob, blinking as she takes in our position on the ground, my legs folded underneath her. "Your legs must be killing you."

"I can't actually feel them anymore, so it's fine."

She giggles and sniffles, quickly climbing off me as she wipes her face with the heels of her hands. "Why didn't you say anything?"

"And interrupt you? I don't think so." I groan as I stretch out my stupid old man legs and my knees that sound like bubble wrap, and Amber kneels beside me, her hands clutched in her lap. I give her a weak smile, and reach out to sweep her hair over her shoulder. "So when did you decide that you didn't want to try to be happy in that life anymore?"

Her gaze darts away from mine, and her hands fidget restlessly in her lap. "It's embarrassing."

"You could never say anything embarrassing to me, honey."

"This is bad, though." Fresh tears well up in her eyes. "It was... when we were in Mexico, over spring break. Ryan and I, after we'd been out one night with our friends. We... went back to our room and... Had sex." Her gaze drops down to her lap. "I... asked him to be rough with me. And he was so tentative about it. He didn't know what to do." Her eyes flash back to mine and she shakes her head. "I didn't force him or anything, it wasn't that I wanted to force him to do that, if he wasn't comfortable, I-"

"Honey, it's ok." I take her hand, raising it to my lips, and brush a kiss against her knuckles. "Just keep talking. I'm not going to judge you."

She sighs, sniffling, and shifts on her legs. "I was

chasing that same feeling I had with you. And I realised it wasn't about the *how,* it was about *who.* Ryan was great, he was perfect on paper, but..." She chews her lip, and clutches my hand tighter. "He wasn't perfect for me. He didn't... line up with me like you did. He made me nervous, I was always on a tightrope with him. But with you..." She leans closer, placing her hand on my cheek. "There's no tightrope. Just hands to hold me. Solid ground under my feet. There's just you. Just us."

I hold her hand to my face, and my own eyes begin to sting. "That last night you were here, I wanted to ask you to stay."

Her eyelashes flutter as her eyes widen. "You did?"

I nod, clearing my throat of the damn lump that's formed. "I wanted to tell you that I want you in my bed every night. That I want to wake up with you. That I... I'll love you forever. But I thought I was being selfish. That I'd ruin your life if I made you stay."

"Maybe I want you to ruin my life." She brings her forehead gently against mine with a soft laugh. "Whatever this is, it makes me happy. And if it makes you happy, too, then everything else is just noise. We can deal with it. But I don't want to walk the tightrope anymore."

"You deserve the bridge, honey."

She smiles at me, more tears cascading down her cheeks, and climbs on top of me. "That was so fucking cheesy."

"A man learns a few things when he watches Hallmark movie marathons to deal with his broken heart," I say with a grin.

Her lips tremble, and more tears stream down her cheeks. "Is that what you did?"

"I missed you." I run my hands up her back and into her

hair. "And I was an idiot who didn't know how to cope with losing you. But I know I don't want to be with anyone else for the rest of my life. Just you. Even if your brothers hunt me down and bury me in the woods. I just want you."

She wraps her arms around my neck, and kisses me deeply, and I don't care that she's not my first, that I'm not hers. She's my last.

"Take me to bed," she whispers against my mouth.

"Yes, ma'am."

———

Amber's brows pinch together, and she whimpers as my tongue traces over her clit.

"Theo, please." Her back bows from the bed.

"Patience, honey." I suck her clit between my lips, and she shoves a hand against her mouth. "I didn't take my time the first time, so now I'm going to."

That first feverish rush was like being straight back in the drugged-up haze I felt with her all those weeks and months ago. We'd barely made it up the stairs, falling to the ground in a tangle of limbs, eventually half-crawling, half-fucking our way to my bed, where Amber just managed to haul her upper body onto the mattress before I sank into her. It was messy, it was hot and sweaty, and I'm sure the neighbours heard us through the open windows.

Don't care. Fucking *worth it*.

But now, an hour later, after more kisses, more telling me I'm an asshole, I want to take my time with my woman. *My woman.* Jesus fucking christ, she's beautiful. Even more beautiful than she was two years ago.

My fingertips brush over the constellation tattoo on her

thigh, and I chuckle against her skin. "And I still want to hear the story about this."

"Oh, y-yeah?" She lets out a strained moan-giggle, her chest pounding in an irregular rhythm as I keep licking and sucking. "F-fuck, *Theo*."

I'm too smug. Too fucking smug. The desperation in her voice, the way her hips rock against my face. She's so needy, and I know she wasn't fucked the way she needed to be since she was with me. *Smug fucking asshole.* Sue me.

"I-I watched that video," she murmurs, her hands on her perfect tits. "Th-that night, after... after him. I watched the video where you - *Ah!*" Her spine goes rigid as I push two fingers inside her, my tongue still circling her swollen clit. "O-oh fuck." She lets out a shaky breath. "I watched the video where you... You made me film us. And the way you said my name, the way you... Oh *fuck*." Her fingers rake through my hair, holding my face to her cunt. "Oh my god, Theo."

"I told you no one can take care of this pussy like me, didn't I?" *SMUG FUCKING ASSHOLE*. But I just grin, rolling my fingertips against her g-spot. "I watched that video too, every single day. Hearing you moan my name like that, honey. You have no idea."

I suck her clit, hard, and she cries out, her toes digging into my back. She's feral, fucking ravenous for more, for me, and Jesus if that isn't the turn-on of the century.

"I love watching you come," she moans, and if the neighbours really can hear us, then godspeed to them. "It does something to me, just... *Oh fuck*." She throws her hands over her head, clawing into the pillow, and she moans loudly, so fucking loudly, her hips rolling her soaked cunt against my face. Her cunt clenches around my fingers, her orgasm sending her arching from the bed, feet planted against my shoulders.

"*Theo*, oh god," she cries. "Fuck, please, I need you."

"I'm right here, honey." I trace my lips along her thigh, gently curling my fingers inside her until she melts into the bed with a long sigh. "I'm not going anywhere."

"You better be." She raises her head from the bed with a breathless laugh. "Up here, right now."

"So bossy," I tease, chuckling against her thigh, then move up over her hips, her stomach, kissing and smelling and tasting her. "How did you get even sexier in the past two years?"

"I guess it's all that *maturity*." She gasps as my tongue teases her hard nipple. "All that getting *older* you keep talking about."

"Bad girl." I suck her nipple into my mouth, rolling my tongue around it, and she sinks her fingers into my hair. "You taste like sunshine."

"Do I?" She sighs as I kiss along her collarbone, up the column of her throat. "That sounds nice."

"It is very nice." I settle over the top of her, and she opens her eyes to gaze into mine. "I don't think I want to leave this bed for a long." I kiss the corner of her mouth, grinning as her lips open eagerly, expecting more. "Long." I kiss the other corner, and it happens again. My sweet, greedy girl. "Time."

With a frustrated groan she wraps her legs around my waist, seizing my face to kiss me, hard and hot, her tongue licking hungrily against mine. I'm pressed right to her entrance, and without breaking the kiss, I sink into her, pushing her thigh back with my hand to open her up more.

She moans and gasps into my mouth, writhing under

me, but the first thrust of my hips sends her still, her lips quivering.

"Is that good for you, honey?" I ask in a low voice, my mouth hovering over hers.

"Y-yes," she murmurs.

I pump again, harder this time, and her jaw clenches as she suppresses a cry.

"Do you know how beautiful you look?" I set a slow rhythm, savouring this, wanting to just feel her stretched around me. "Like a dream. Like the best fucking dream I've ever had."

She whimpers as she nudges her leg to my side, and I sling it over my shoulder.

"*Oh, FUCK*!" She screams and moans so loud that the cops are going to pull up any second. "Shit, Theo, holy *shit*."

I pull back a little, even though being so deep inside her is like heaven.

"Is that too deep for you?"

She shakes her head frantically, her hand clawing into my bicep. "Fuck, no, no, just... Oh god." Her stomach contracts, and when I sink back into her, I swear I'm going to fucking detonate.

"*Fuck*," I moan, and her lips twitch into a grin. She knows just how good she feels for me. And because she feels so good, I can't help but fuck her mercilessly, chasing the high. Fuck it, we can do this all night, all day tomorrow, all damn week until the real world calls us back.

She's coated in sweat, and she's mesmerising underneath me. I will never get tired of the way her body moves, the way it feels. I dip my head to kiss her, and she leans up eagerly, propping herself up on an elbow, panting against my lips.

She looks down between us, watching me sink into her

over and over. "I love... watching you fuck me." She squeezes her eyes shut, and gasps in a breath. "Oh shit. Theo, I'm..." Her head falls back, her perfect tits bouncing with each thrust. She cries out, then she's coming again, unraveling around me, her back curving and her hips bucking to meet me.

I drop her leg from my shoulder, covering her body with mine, and grind into her as she rides out her climax. I breathe hard into her neck, heat pulling and tearing at every vein in my body. My hands find hers, our fingers entwined, and just as I groan, and that first hot jet of cum erupts deep inside her, she claims my mouth, biting at my lips, stroking my tongue with hers.

I shudder as I come down, and she kisses my jaw, her fingers flexing between mine, telling me she loves me, *she loves me, only me.*

Bliss. Ecstasy. And I was going to pass this up.

Fucking idiot.

When I roll off her to lie beside her, sweat soaking us both, she sighs, and feathers the backs of her fingers along my arm.

"Your dad is going to kill me," I say, and we both laugh.

"He'll be fine." She turns onto her side, caressing my chest. "I had a thought."

"Oh yeah?"

She nods. "I want you to come to my grandparents' place tomorrow."

My eyebrows shoot up. "Are you serious?"

"Yep. I think if you're going to meet anyone first, and we announce this, it should be to them."

"And why is that?"

Amber grins widely. "My grandpa is 20 years older than my grandma."

I run a hand over my face and laugh. "Of course he is."

"*And.*" Amber leans over me, and folds her hands on my chest. "To make it truly scandalous, she was 19 when they met."

"Your granddaddy was a bad man." I run my fingers through her hair with a chuckle. "But they made it work I guess."

"Married 54 years." Amber rests her chin on top of her folded hands, still gazing at me. "Still madly in love."

"Good for them." I tuck my hand behind my head. "Alright. If you think your parents are less likely to murder me if your grandparents are cool, then let's do it."

"And then..." Amber trails off, and her face is a little less confident now.

"And then?" I raise an eyebrow. "What then, honey?"

"And then..." She sits up, sweeping her hair from her neck. "Move to Boston with me?"

I sit up too, cupping her face gently with my hand. "You mean that?"

She nods, smiling shyly. "I do."

I pull her to me, and kiss her. "Yes."

She meets my eyes, her face flooded with happiness so pure it makes my heart pound. "Really?"

"Of course." I pull her on top of me, and she drapes her arms around my neck. "Wherever you go, I go. We'll make it work."

She closes her eyes, and leans her forehead against mine with a sigh. "I'm so glad I got up the courage to come over that day."

"Me, too, honey." *Me. Fucking. Too.*

ACKNOWLEDGMENTS

This book wouldn't exist with my amazing PA, Deana.

I was knee-deep in writer's block, sitting in front of the computer and weeping every day, and she told me to write a novella. "Something short and smutty you don't care about, 20k words, throw it on KU, and move on."

Well.... At 57k words, I guess I didn't quite manage a novella. But it still broke my writer's block, and created two characters I adore.

My beta readers, who were thrilled with Theo and Amber and wanted more, thank you.

The amazing artists I got to work with, who created the most beautiful art of Theo and Amber - thank you.

And to the readers who preordered this smutty little book, who were so excited about it, who cheered and hyped in my comments on social media - thank you.

ABOUT THE AUTHOR

RD Baker blames her love of all things dark and twisted on too much time spent unsupervised with books back in the 90s - and VC Andrews.

She lives in the Blue Mountains, Australia, on Darug/Gundungurra Land, with her family.

Want to keep up with all the latest updates? Sign up for RD's newsletter at rdbakerwrites.com!

ALSO BY RD BAKER

Unseen

Fracture

Afflicted

The Lost Heirs Series

A Realm of Dark Fury

The Shadow Drawn Series

The Shadow and The Draw

The Earth and The Flame

Writing as Rihannon Baker

No One Else Ever

Clearwater

Endlessly